ARE YOU A BASEBALL FAN?

If you are, this book is for you! Baseball has a long and glorious history, filled with the exploits of great teams, incredible superstars, and amazing athletes. These are their tales—some from the past, and some as new as last season! Along with these highlights, you'll be treated to photographs straight from *Sports Illustrated* that make you feel like you're right down there on the diamond and a part of the action. *Sports Illustrated* is known for its coverage of the finest moments in sports. Now, here are baseball's finest moments—just waiting for you!

Books by Bill Gutman

Sports Illustrated BASEBALL'S RECORD BREAKERS
Sports Illustrated GREAT MOMENTS IN BASEBALL
Sports Illustrated GREAT MOMENTS IN PRO FOOTBALL
Sports Illustrated PRO FOOTBALL'S RECORD BREAKERS
Sports Illustrated STRANGE AND AMAZING BASEBALL STORIES
Sports Illustrated STRANGE AND AMAZING FOOTBALL STORIES
BASEBALL SUPER TEAMS
BASEBALL'S HOT NEW STARS
BO JACKSON: A BIOGRAPHY
FOOTBALL SUPER TEAMS
GREAT SPORTS UPSETS
MICHAEL JORDAN: A BIOGRAPHY
PRO SPORTS CHAMPIONS
STRANGE AND AMAZING WRESTLING STORIES

Available from ARCHWAY Paperbacks

Sports Illustrated

GREAT MOMENTS
IN BASEBALL

Bill Gutman

AN ARCHWAY PAPERBACK
Published by POCKET BOOKS

New York   London   Toronto   Sydney   Tokyo   Singapore

Photos courtesy of *Sports Illustrated;* Heinz Kluetmeier: p. 12; Neil Leifer: pp. 63, 89; Walter Iooss Jr.: p. 103; George Tiedemann: p. 119; Manny Millan: p. 118; Bill Smith: p. 108. Photos on pp. 3, 25, 36, 45, 48, 54, 57, 77 courtesy of AP/Wide World Photos.

AN ARCHWAY PAPERBACK *Original*

An Archway Paperback published by
POCKET BOOKS, a division of Simon & Schuster Inc.
1230 Avenue of the Americas, New York, NY 10020

ISBN: 0-671-67914-7

First Archway Paperback printing April 1987

10 9 8 7 6 5 4

AN ARCHWAY PAPERBACK and colophon are
registered trademarks of Simon & Schuster Inc.

SPORTS ILLUSTRATED is a registered trademark
of Time Inc.

Printed in the U.S.A.

IL 5+

Contents

By More Than an Eyelash

Without a doubt, one of the greatest hitters the game of baseball has ever known was Ted Williams. The man they called the "Splendid Splinter" played for the Boston Red Sox from 1939 to 1960, and racked up the numbers that put him right up there with the other greats of the game. Start with a lifetime batting average of .344, add to that 521 home runs and more than 1,800 runs batted in, and you can fully understand why Ted Williams is a member of the Hall of Fame.

In fact, there are very few young ballplayers today who wouldn't be more than satisfied to complete their careers with something close to the stats of Ted Williams. Yet the amazing thing was that Williams compiled his numbers despite missing nearly five full seasons to military service. He lost 1943–44–45 when he served during World War II, and then was recalled during the Korean War and served for most of 1952 and 1953.

Had Ted Williams played during these five peak seasons, his accomplishments would have been considerably greater. As things stand, the brash and often outspoken Williams produced more than his share of great moments, from the earliest days of his career right up to his very last at bat in the major leagues, when he smashed his 521st and final home run. It was a classic way to bow out.

But between that final, dramatic home run and his 1939 debut as a skinny, 6'4", twenty-year-old, there were feuds with reporters and the fans in Boston which some say left the Splendid Splinter a somewhat bitter man. For instance, to the end, he refused to tip his cap to the hometown fans following one of his many home runs. Yet he was always a gamer who gave everything to the sport he loved.

Williams believed in practice, and when he got done with that—more practice. He could hit baseballs for hours on end, often putting blisters on top of blisters. And because he considered hitting a baseball the most difficult single skill to master in all sports, he often criticized young players for not practicing enough.

It was obvious from the first that the lanky outfielder was destined for greatness. Playing for Minneapolis in the American Association in 1938, Williams won the triple crown with a .366 batting average, 43 home runs, and 142 runs batted in. That prompted a call from the Red Sox, and the following spring he was a major leaguer.

Though he only weighed in the vicinity of 150 pounds his rookie year (he would later fill out to a solid 200), he was already all hitter. By the time the season ended Ted Williams was hitting .327, had 31 homers, and a league-leading 145 RBIs. Not a bad debut. He showed it was no fluke the next year, hitting .344, which was to be his lifetime mark. Then came his third season, 1941. It was a year when Ted Williams would produce one of the greatest moments in baseball history.

A young Ted Williams follows the flight of yet another hit during the 1941 season. In only his third season in the majors, he went on to hit .406. He was the last player in baseball to hit over the magic .400 mark.

The Splinter had high hopes for a big year, but his progress was slowed when he chipped a bone in his ankle during spring training. So for the first couple of weeks of the season he was used mainly as a pinch hitter. Yet he never stopped practicing, never stopped swinging the bat, and by the time he was fit for full-time duty, he was in a good groove, where he remained.

All during the long summer his average stayed over the .400 mark. A slump or even a mild dry period, something most hitters experience during the course of a season, never happened, and Ted's average continued above .400. Yet it took awhile for the excitement to build simply because the 1941 baseball season was an extraordinary one in several ways.

While the Splendid Splinter was whacking the ball at better than a .400 clip, another great ballplayer of that era, Joe DiMaggio, was creating one of baseball's greatest records. From May 15 to July 17, the famed Yankee Clipper hit safely in an amazing 56 consecutive games, setting a record that stands to this day, a record some experts feel will never be broken.

It was only after DiMag's great streak ended that attention began focusing on Williams. After all, the .400 hitter was a dying breed. The last time it had been accomplished prior to 1941 was in 1930, when Bill Terry of the New York Giants batted .401. Gone were the days when players like Ty Cobb, Rogers Hornsby, George Sisler, Nap Lajoie, and Shoeless Joe Jackson made a business of hitting .400.

But when Ted was still hitting the ball at a better-than-.400 clip as August turned to September, baseball fans realized the young slugger was mounting a very serious threat. With his average still at .413 by mid-

September, it looked as if he'd make it, hands down. That's when the pressure really took hold. Each game was more difficult, with the pitchers bearing down and trying to stop the Splinter.

What it came down to was this. The Red Sox's season ended with a doubleheaded at Philadelphia. Williams' average coming into those final two games was exactly .399955. Rounded out, it would go in the books as .400 even. Manager Joe Cronin then made Ted an offer. He could sit out the doubleheader and assure himself of a .400 average in the record books.

But Williams wouldn't hear of it. He didn't want to be known as a player who made .400 by an eyelash, who had to have his average rounded out to make it. He practically demanded to play. Then the night before, with the pressure coming down all around him, he went out with equipment man Johnny Orlando and just walked. Orlando later estimated that the two must have walked ten miles. But when the doubleheader rolled around, Ted Williams was ready for his great moment.

As he came to bat for the first time, he got some advice from home plate umpire Bill McGowan, then a warning from A's catcher Frank Hayes.

"A batter has got to be loose if he wants to hit .400," McGowan said while dusting off the plate. "He's got to be loose."

But as Ted dug in to face righthander Dick Fowler, catcher Hayes wished him luck, then added: "We're not gonna give you any gifts, Ted. Mr. Mack (A's longtime manager Connie Mack) told us if we let up on you, he'll run us all out of baseball."

So it wouldn't be easy. But Ted wasn't one to duck a challenge. He promptly smacked a Fowler offering be-

5

tween first and second for a solid single. He was now a .400 hitter without having to round off the average. He could have easily come out of the game right then and there. But he didn't. And the next time he faced Fowler he poled a long home run into the rightfield stands.

Brimming with confidence, Williams next faced lefty reliever Porter Vaughn, a pitcher he had never hit against before. It didn't matter. He singled off Vaughn and repeated it with another base hit several innings later. Four hits under tremendous pressure and his average was safely over the .400 mark. He had made baseball history. Yet he still wouldn't sit, insisting on starting the second game of the twin bill as well.

Bearing down once more, the Splinter cracked a double and single in game two, giving him six hits in eight trips for the day. From a .399955 average going in, Ted Williams had wound up the day batting .406. It was one of baseball's great moments and great clutch performances.

It certainly wasn't the end of the great moments for Ted Williams. There were many others, like the home run he hit off Rip Sewell's famed eephus pitch (a high, floating blooper) in the 1946 All-Star Game, his various comebacks following injuries and seasons lost to military service, and the final home run in his farewell game.

Through it all, he remained an amazing hitter. In 1957, at the age of thirty-nine, this astounding baseball star hit .388, coming within five hits of a second .400 season. What's more, he did it with a second-half hitting spree that saw him bat at a .453 clip in the final months of the season. It seemed that no one could get him out.

He won his sixth and last batting crown a year later, hitting .328 at the age of forty, then played two more seasons before retiring. Yet with all his great moments, his final-day binge against the A's in 1941 remains a standout. It not only enabled him to become a .400 hitter by considerably more than an eyelash, but it also made him the last of a breed. Because in the nearly fifty years that have passed since Ted Williams hit .406, no major league player has ever hit .400 again.

Mr. October

It's a nickname that makes Reggie Jackson proud. *Mr. October.* It signifies clutch performance, a gamer, someone who produces when it's for all the marbles. *Mr. October.* That's World Series time. October. And there's no better time for a ballplayer to produce great moments. Despite being outspoken, boastful, and often controversial, Reggie Jackson has been a walking, talking great moment. He's always backed up the words with deeds.

Early in his career, Reggie summed up his approach to the game, a philosophy that would lead to the eventual title of Mr. October.

"There's nothing better than hitting a ball hard, real hard," he said. "Just the feel of it, the sound of it, everything. It's beautiful. And I love going to the ballpark, putting on that uniform, then playing in front of a packed house. There's nothing like it."

That's what really turned Reggie Jackson on. The packed house, the big game, the chance to hit a ball hard, real hard. A muscular lefthanded hitter with a home run swing, Reggie signed with the then Kansas City A's right off the Arizona State University campus in 1966. He played briefly with Kansas City in 1967, then became a regular when the team moved to Oakland a year later.

A year after that, in 1969, young Reggie Jackson hit the spotlight for the first time. He went on a batting tear that saw him belt 39 home runs by the end of July. It looked as if he would mount a serious challenge to the home run record of 61, set by Roger Maris in 1961. But he tailed off in the final months to finish with 47 round-trippers and 118 RBIs. Yet he began to look like one of baseball's young supersluggers.

When he tailed off in 1970, there were those ready to call him a one-year wonder. But he began to recover his form in 1971 and made it to the All-Star Game as a last-minute substitute for an injured starter. He was on the bench as the National League took a 3–0 lead going to the bottom of the third inning.

With some 50,000 fans on hand at Detroit's Tiger Stadium, Reggie got the call as a pinch hitter with a runner on first. This was center stage, the kind of situation he loved, and Reggie Jackson dug in to face righthander Dock Ellis. Ellis seemed in command as he quickly got two strikes on the young slugger. Then he tried to slip a fastball past the pinch hitter.

Reggie was set and took his compact, but powerful swing. The sound of solid contact was unmistakable, and the ball left the bat as if propelled by a rocket, rising majestically toward right-center field. A pair of future Hall of Fame outfielders, Hank Aaron and Willie Mays, just stood and watched as the ball sailed over the fence. And it was still rising!

For a split second, it appeared headed right out of Tiger Stadium, but it slammed into a generator box at the top of a light tower in right center. The tower was more than 500 feet from home plate. There's no telling how far the ball would have gone if it had sailed out unobstructed. The huge crowd was stunned to near silence by the blast. Not very many in the stadium had ever seen a ball hit so hard. Even many of the players were awed by Jackson's power. And his shot paved the way for a 6–4 American League comeback victory.

It was Reggie Jackson's first real great moment, but far from his last. By the time the 1977 season rolled around Reggie was a veteran and one of the slugging stars of the game. And while he had helped lead the Oakland A's to three straight World Series triumphs, his relationship with A's owner Charles O. Finley was always a rocky one. A free agent following the 1976 season, Reggie decided to move on. He signed a big five-year pact with the New York Yankees.

The Yanks had a powerful team and had made it into the World Series in 1976. But they were swept by the Cincinnati Reds that year and flamboyant owner George Steinbrenner didn't want that to happen again. Among the new players joining the team for 1977 was Reggie Jackson. This was the Yankees of Munson, Rivers, Chambliss, Nettles, Piniella, Dent, Guidry, Gullett, Torrez, Hunter, and Lyle, the whole crew managed by the volatile Billy Martin.

It was quite a collection of egos, and they didn't always mesh. As usual, Reggie liked being the center of attention. Early in the season he clashed with the late Thurman Munson, who was the Yankee leader at the time. Later, there were problems between Reggie and manager Martin. Much of it stemmed from Reggie wanting to bat cleanup and the manager moving him around in the lineup.

Finally, on August 10, Reggie got his wish. He was batting fourth and he went on a late-season tear to help the club win 39 of its final 52 games and sweep to another A.L. Eastern Division title. Reggie finished the regular season with a .286 average, 32 homers, and a team-leading 110 RBIs. Once again he had spoken his mind, claiming he'd produce in the cleanup spot. And once more he was good to his word. He had.

What is all this leading to? With Reggie, it can only be another great moment. And in 1977, he had the best stage of all, the World Series. The Yanks were there once more after whipping the Kansas City Royals in the playoffs. Now they would be facing the Los Angeles Dodgers for the championship.

It was an interesting series, both on and off the field. As had become the norm, the Yankee players sniped at each other and at management throughout the series, with a number of players demanding to be traded and claiming they wouldn't return for another season in what had become known as the Bronx Zoo.

But the club could play ball. Game one at Yankee Stadium went 12 innings before the New Yorkers won it, 4–3. The Dodgers evened things with a 6–1 victory in the second game, but the Yanks came through, 5–3, in the first game played at Dodger Stadium. They led 2–1 in games, and it was almost Reggie time.

It started in game four. Reggie had been hitting well during the entire series, and in the fourth game belted a long homer to help the Yanks win it, 4–2. Though the Dodgers won the fifth easily, 10–4, Reggie hit another circuit shot, his second of the series. Now the teams returned to Yankee Stadium for game six. The New Yorkers needed one more victory to wrap things up

In one of his most dramatic great moments, Reggie Jackson belted three homers on three consecutive pitches off of three consecutive pitchers in the sixth game of the 1977 World Series. His performance helped the Yankees triumph in the Series.

and the stage was set for one of baseball's great moments.

Mike Torrez was on the mound for the Yanks against Burt Hooten, who had beaten the Bombers in game two. The Dodgers got off the mark with a pair of runs in the first, but the Yanks came right back in the second when Reggie walked and Chris Chambliss belted a long homer, tying the game. The Dodgers broke the tie with a run in the third, but now the complexion of the game was about to change as Reggie Jackson prepared to take over.

In the bottom of the fourth, Munson singled and Reggie came up. He dug in and Hooten delivered. Boom! Reggie nailed the first pitch and drove it high and deep into the rightfield stands for a two-run homer, giving the Yanks a 4–3 lead.

It was a 5–3 game when Jackson came up again in the fifth. This time Mickey Rivers was on base and Elias Sosa pitching. Once again Reggie went after the first pitch. The crack was unmistakable, and the ball rocketed on a line into the lower rightfield seats. Home run number two, and the Bombers were comfortably ahead, 7–3. The fans roared as Jackson circled the bases in his familiar home run trot.

When Reggie came up again in the eighth, it was still 7–3 with the Yanks well on their way to another world title. As a way of thanking him, the huge crowd began chanting, REGGIE . . . REGGIE . . . REGGIE. The big slugger loved it. He was facing knuckleballer Charlie Hough and he wanted nothing better than to give the fans an encore.

Hough's first pitch was a flutterball and Reggie timed it perfectly, hitting a high, arching, majestic shot to deep, deep center. The ball sailed into the faraway bleachers with plenty of room to spare. Reggie circled the bases once more, slowly, savoring the moment. The fans didn't want it to end, either, for they knew they had just seen baseball history made.

The Yanks won the game and the series, 8–4, as Reggie Jackson became the toast of the town. His three homers in one game tied a record set by the one and only Babe Ruth, and Reggie's five homers in the series enabled him to carve his own niche in the record books. What's more, his three homers had come on just three pitches, and off three different pitchers. It was an amazing performance.

But then again, Reggie Jackson has always been an amazing baseball player. After his five-year pact with the Yanks was over, the club let him go and he signed with California, where he continued to produce the big moments. Early in the 1986 season, he belted his 537th lifetime homer, enabling him to pass Hall of Famer Mickey Mantle and go into sixth place on the all-time home run list. Still another great moment for the man they'll always call Mr. October.

Throw 'Em the Thing

Since its inception in 1933, the All-Star Game has been one of baseball's bright showcases. The Midsummer Classic, as it's often called, gives fans a chance to see their favorite stars competing in an exhibition game that pits the National League against the American League. And while it's an equally enjoyable time for fans and players alike, the pride of these top-notch performers often leads to memorable moments.

It started in the very first All-Star Game in 1933. Fittingly, the American League won it on a two-run homer off the bat of the aging Babe Ruth, nearing the end of his playing days, but still more than capable of producing a great moment. And there would be many more, with the best players of their time often rising to the occasion in a game that didn't really count.

But of all the great All-Star moments, perhaps the greatest occurred in just the second game, the 1934 contest. The American League was a heavy favorite as their starting lineup was dominated by great hitters. In fact, the starting eight players in that game are all members of the Hall of Fame today.

National League pitchers would be facing the likes of Charley Gehringer, Heinie Manush, Babe Ruth, Lou

Gehrig, Jimmie Foxx, Al Simmons, Joe Cronin, and Bill Dickey. There probably wasn't a pitcher alive who would relish facing that kind of wrecking crew. But somebody had to start the game and the task went to the New York Giants' ace hurler, King Carl Hubbell.

A late-blooming lefthander, the tall, angular Hubbell was thirty-one-years-old at the time of the 1934 All-Star Game, but he was just entering the peak years of his career. He had thrown a no-hitter back in 1929, but didn't have his first 20-game season until 1933, when he was 23–12 with 10 shutouts. He also pitched a classic 1–0 victory over the Cardinals that year, a game that went 18 innings. Hubbell pitched them all and showed his great control by not walking a single batter.

The 6′ 1″, 175-pound southpaw was not an over-powering pitcher. He did have fine control, but his success was built on his ability to master a single pitch. In the early days of baseball it was called a fadeaway and in Hubbell's day many called it the butterfly. Today, most fans recognize this pitch by the name screwball, or screwjie.

Basically, it's a reverse curve. A lefthander's curve ball breaks in toward a righthanded hitter. The pitcher throws it by turning his wrist in a counterclockwise motion. The screwball is thrown just the opposite way, turning the wrist out, or in a clockwise direction. Not too many pitchers have really mastered the screwball. It's thrown with an unnatural motion and puts tremendous strain on the elbow.

But Carl Hubbell had complete command of the screwjie, and it helped him win 253 games during his big league career. He eventually paid the price of throwing this peculiar pitch, suffering elbow problems that limited his effectiveness in the final years of his career. And years after his retirement, people who saw him often wondered why his left hand turned outward when he walked. It was from years of throwing the screwball.

None of that mattered in 1934. The man the Giants called the Meal Ticket was slated to start against the big bats of the American League. And in spite of the fact that King Carl was en route to another 20-game season, and the year before had won a pair of World Series games without surrendering a run, the A.L. hitters were confident.

The game was played at Hubbell's home field, the Polo Grounds in New York, and the lefty got a big cheer as he took the mound for the opening inning. Yet none of the more than 48,000 fans who jammed the old park under Coogan's Bluff knew that a truly great moment was just a hair's breath away.

Whether Hubbell was nervous or just being careful was hard to say. But the leadoff hitter, Charley Gehringer, promptly drove a curve to center for a base hit. Hubbell then faced Heinie Manush and walked him on a three-two pitch. Because of the short dimensions of the Polo Grounds down each foul line, Hubbell was trying to keep the ball away from the hitters and getting too fine with his pitches. Now there were two on and none out, with the heart of the A.L. batting order coming up. It called for a conference at the mound.

With infielders Bill Terry, Frankie Frisch, Travis Jackson, and Pie Traynor gathered around, King Carl pawed at the dirt nervously. But catcher Gabby Hartnett of the Cubs broke the ice and took charge.

17

"No more pitching carefully, Hub," he said. "Throw 'em the thing. It always gets me out."

With the legendary Babe Ruth stepping to the plate, Hubbell knew what he had to do. He started the Babe off with a fastball off the plate. Then he threw three straight screwballs and the Babe took the third one for a called strike three. Now up came Lou Gehrig of the Yanks.

Still going with the screwjie, Hubbell fanned Gehrig on four pitches as Larrupin' Lou hit nothing but air. Next came Foxx, old Double X, who blasted 534 home runs in his great career. As he approached the plate, Gehrig was leaving, and Lou supposedly told Jimmie not to wait for Hubbell to bring the ball up, because he wouldn't. That meant the screwjie was working to perfection, breaking down low.

Unlike Ruth and Gehrig, Foxx batted from the right side. Because Hubbell and Hartnett were concentrating so hard on the hitter, Gehringer and Manush were able to execute a double steal, putting themselves both in scoring position. But it didn't really matter as Hubbell then threw three more sharp-breaking screwballs to Foxx and Double X went down swinging.

Once again the fans roared. They had just seen their own Giants' hero mow down three of the greatest hitters in baseball history. But Hubbell wasn't finished yet. When he returned to the mound in the second inning, he continued to throw his specialty. The great Al Simmons was up first and Hubbell struck him out! Then came Joe Cronin. Same result, another strikeout. King Carl had just set an All-Star Game record with five consecutive strikeouts, and they had come against five future Hall of Fame hitters.

Bill Dickey broke the string with a single, but Hubbell promptly fanned opposing pitcher Lefty Gomez to end the inning. And when he left the game after his three-inning stint, the National Leaguers had a 4–0 lead. Unfortunately, the other N.L. pitchers weren't as successful as the Meal Ticket, and the American League came back to win it, 9–7.

But National League fans still left with a prideful gleam in their eye. They had witnessed an incredible pitching feat, a great moment that will always be a part of baseball lore.

Say Hey Goes a Long Way

Ask any baseball fan in the 1950s or 1960s what "Say Hey" meant and you would get a quick answer. Willie Mays. The Say Hey Kid was the nickname of the most exciting ballplayer of his generation. Sure, people might argue that Willie wasn't the absolute best. Mickey Mantle, Henry Aaron, even Roberto Clemente might get votes for the best. But the most exciting? It had to be Mays.

That's because Willie played the game with flair, with a boyish exuberance that never seemed to diminish. And he could do it all—run, hit, throw, field, steal bases, hit with power, and create great moments. When he chased a fly or ran the bases, his cap invariably came flying off. In the outfield he used an unconventional basket catch, grabbing the ball at his waist, a maneuver most outfielders wouldn't even attempt. Yet Willie was the most sure-handed outfielder of his time.

More than anything else, Willie Mays loved to play baseball. As a youngster with the New York Giants, Willie could often be found playing stickball on the streets of New York when the Giants didn't have a game. His nickname came from the happy greeting he gave people. "Say, hey," Willie would quip.

His philosophy regarding the game was simple. "Play ball in the way that's most natural for you," he said. "But get out and play every day. You got to work at it day in and day out if you ever want to be good."

Willie had played every minute he could from the time he was a young boy, and he was rewarded by reaching the majors in 1951 at the age of twenty. He was a New York Giant until the franchise moved to San Francisco following the 1957 season. There are some who have said that the Mays legend would have been even greater if the team had stayed in New York, that the people of San Francisco never really appreciated Willie as much as the fans in New York.

Mays closed his Hall of Fame career in 1973, as a .300 lifetime hitter who collected more than 3,000 hits, and was the third leading home-run hitter of all time with 660 round-trippers. The great moments are just too numerous to count, but there are many Mays fans who still think the greatest of Willie's great moments came toward the beginning of his career, in the 1954 World Series.

The Giants had called him up three years earlier. He had spent the first month or so of the 1951 season tearing up minor league pitching at Minneapolis, where he was hitting an incredible .477. Giants manager Leo Durocher summoned the fleet youngster and immediately installed him in centerfield.

Willie's first major league hit was a home run off the great Warren Spahn. He hit only .274 with 20 round-trippers his rookie year, but he was involved in one of the greatest pennant races of all time. That was the year the Giants came from way back to catch the old Brooklyn Dodgers at the wire. Then in a playoff game,

Bobby Thomson hit the famous shot heard 'round the world, the dramatic homer that won it for the Jints.

There was a "subway series" that year, with the Giants losing to the New York Yankees in six games. But Willie had gained a wealth of experience and was touted as a coming superstar of the game. Only it would have to wait a couple of years. With the Korean War heating up, Willie was called into the army and spent the next two years serving Uncle Sam. In the spring of 1954 he was back and ready to play.

The Giants needed him badly. The Dodgers had regained the top spot while Mays was away, winning both in 1952 and 1953, with the Giants sinking as low as fifth place in '53. But it was quickly obvious that with Willie Mays in the lineup, the Giants were a different team. Willie was simply amazing from start to finish, having a season most players just dream about.

He won the batting title with a .345 average, belted 41 home runs, and drove home 110 runs. For his efforts, he was awarded the National League's Most Valuable Player prize. And what's more important, he helped his team recapture the N.L. pennant. So the Giants had another crack at winning the world's championship.

Only this time they wouldn't be playing the Yankees. After setting a record with five straight pennants and World Series triumphs, the Yanks had been dethroned by the Cleveland Indians. In fact, the Tribe had won a record 111 games in 1954 and had a balanced, powerful team with an outstanding pitching staff. The Giants, by contrast, had won just 97 games in the regular season and the Indians were installed as heavy favorites in the Series.

The Series opened at the Polo Grounds in New York with Cleveland's 23-game winner, Bob Lemon, opposing veteran Sal Maglie, who had won just 14. And in the very first inning it looked as if the Indians would make quick work of the man they called the Barber.

Maglie plunked leadoff batter Al Smith with a pitch, and American League batting champ, Bobby Avila, followed with a single. Then Maglie settled down to retire the next two hitters, but veteran first baseman Vic Wertz upset the apple cart by poling a long triple over the head of rightfielder Don Mueller, scoring two runs. The Indians had broken on top.

Fortunately, Maglie then got into a good groove, and after the Giants tied it with a pair in the third, the game became a pitchers' duel. The score stayed knotted at two each until the eighth. Then the veteran Maglie seemed to tire. He walked Larry Doby and then Al Rosen reached first on an infield hit. Manager Durocher brought in lefthander Don Liddle to face the dangerous Wertz, who already had three hits on the day.

Because Wertz was hitting the ball so well, Willie Mays took a couple of steps back in centerfield. The Polo Grounds was a baseball relic, a monument to the past, and its dimensions were perhaps the strangest in the game. The distances down both foul lines were very short, yet centerfield was the deepest in baseball. The clubhouse in dead center was some 480 feet from home plate, and the bleachers in left-center and right-center were more than 460 feet from home. As of 1954, only one player, Joe Adcock of the Braves, had ever hit a homer into those bleachers.

Now Vic Wertz dug in against Don Liddle, as both Cleveland runners led off base. Liddle's first pitch was right down the pipe and Wertz swung. The big first baseman, who was to crack more than 250 home runs in his career, never hit one harder than this. The ball took off toward deep right-center field. And at almost the same instant the ball took off, so did Willie Mays in center.

It was as if Willie was operating with built-in radar, as if he knew immediately where the ball was going to come down. Once he turned his back on home plate and started running, he didn't look again. Even Willie didn't think he would catch up with the drive, but he kept going at full speed.

As he neared the distant bleachers, and with the roar of more than 52,000 fans ringing in his ears, Willie reached out with both arms and the ball descended over his left shoulder and settled in his glove. He was some 460 feet from home plate when he made his incredible catch.

Then, without pausing even a split second to savor the moment, the marvelous centerfielder spun around backward and unleashed a powerful throw back toward second base. The ball reached second sacker Davey Williams on a single hop. While Doby tagged and went to third, he was prevented from scoring. The stunned Rosen didn't even try for second. He just retreated to first and, like everyone else, wondered how any human being could have made such a catch.

When the next two Cleveland hitters were retired without a run scoring, it became obvious that Mays' catch saved the game. It was still 2–2 after nine, and in the 10th, pinch hitter Dusty Rhodes belted a three-run

Willie Mays makes one of the most electrifying catches of all time, saving the first game of the 1954 World Series for the Giants.

shot that just cleared the short wall in right and gave the Giants a 5–2 victory.

From there, the Giants went on to sweep the Indians in four straight, winning the Series in a major upset. Willie Mays continued to play outstanding baseball, as he would for his entire long career. But of all the great plays and great moments he would produce, none could really top that incredible catch that saved game one of the 1954 World Series. It is a moment remembered, savored, and still talked about today.

Lefty's Most Incredible Season

When a pitcher wins more than 300 games in his career, there are a number of conclusions that can safely be drawn on the strength of that monumental feat alone. The pitcher was undoubtedly a superstar of his era, a hurler who was consistently outstanding over a period of many years. He was most likely a record setter, a player who created and produced many great moments during his successful career.

Steve Carlton, the big lefthander with the sharp-breaking slider, qualifies eminently for all of the above. Not only has the man they call Lefty won more than 300 games, but he also ranks second behind Nolan Ryan on the all-time strikeout list. Big and strong, Lefty has been a workhorse performer since the late 1960s.

Yet of all Steve Carlton's accomplishments, there is one thing that stands out. It was not just a great moment, but a great moment that lasted an entire season. The year was 1972, and Steve was coming off his first 20-victory campaign, having gone 20–9 in 1971.

He was with the St. Louis Cardinals then, had been for his entire career up to that time. And after winning

20 big ones, he felt the Cards would want him for a long time to come. The problem was, they didn't want him at *his* price. They wanted him at *their* price. Steve suddenly found himself at a huge contract impasse. He still hoped it would be resolved, but in February of 1972, he was told that he had been traded to the Philadelphia Phillies.

News of the trade was a shock. The Cardinals seemed to be perennial contenders. In fact, Steve had pitched for them in a pair of World Series, in 1967 and 1968. He liked being at or near the top, as most ballplayers do. But the Phils? They were something else, indeed. In 1971, they had finished dead last in the National League's Eastern Division with a 67–95 mark.

The team had some promising youngsters, such as shortstop Larry Bowa, outfielder Greg Luzinski, and third baseman Mike Schmidt. But there were just too many gaps, too many marginal players. The club couldn't expect to do much better in 1972. Still, once he accepted the fact that he had been traded, Steve Carlton came in with a positive attitude. He also found that his sharp-breaking slider, which had been an elusive pitch his last couple of years in St. Louis, was back and was once again a formidable weapon.

Surprisingly, the Phils got off to a quick start in '72. They won 11 of their first 17 games and Steve Carlton had 6 of those 17 decisions. He was 5–1 and seemed on his way to a big year. Then, two things happened—one expected, one not expected. The expected was that the team went into a tailspin, losing 19 of its next 26 games. The unexpected was that Steve Carlton also seemed to fold up.

28

Lefty dropped five straight decisions, giving him a losing record of 5–6. But a closer look showed that it wasn't all because of poor pitching. During the five losses the Phils managed to score only a meager total of 10 runs! Very few pitchers can win with support like that. Some observers figured it would be a pattern that would repeat itself all year. Steve wouldn't get any support, would lose a lot of tough games, and might even become discouraged and throw in the towel.

One reason for that feeling was that in the fifth loss, Steve was beaten by the New York Mets, 7–0, in a game where his pitching was considerably less than impressive. Shortly after that game, the club made a change, firing both the manager and general manager. Director of Player Personnel Paul Owens became the interim manager. Unfortunately, the players remained the same.

But then something started to happen, something that would continue for the rest of the season, something that is unbelievable, even to this day. Steve Carlton began to win. But there was more to it than that. He was winning big. He was awesome, untouchable, all the adjectives that can be used to describe a pitcher in the midst of an incredible season.

The Phils were the same. When Carlton wasn't on the mound, they were horrible, without a doubt the worst team in baseball that year. But with the big lefthander pitching, something of a transformation came over the rest of the team as well. Young outfielder Greg Luzinski explained:

"When Steve was pitching, we *knew* we were going to be in the ballgame. We knew we had a chance to win.

29

It was a good feeling because we didn't have it very often, only about once in four days."

Once in four days was when Steve Carlton was pitching. And was he ever pitching. His winning streak reached 5, then 10, and finally 14 by mid-August. That gave Steve an amazing 19–6 record for the year, and he was leading the league in most major pitching categories. His winning percentage at the time was .760. Yet even with his 19 victories, the Phils as a team had a winning percentage of only .381.

Only six other pitchers in baseball history had won 20 games with last-place teams, but a number of them had also lost many games. For instance, a pitcher named Irving Young had won 20 for the last-place Boston Braves in 1905, but at the same time Young lost 21. Carlton's case was different. Paul Owens noticed a big change in everyone when Steve was pitching.

"You could feel that everything out there was different when he was on the mound," Owens said. "The players would perform differently and I'd even manage differently. It was Steve's charisma, the feeling of confidence everyone had when he was out there."

In one game during his win streak, Steve shut down the hard-hitting Pittsburgh Pirates, a team with five regulars hitting over .300. Lefty won on a three-hit shutout, after which Pittsburgh slugger Willie Stargell made his now-classic comment: "Hitting Steve tonight," Stargell said, "was like drinking coffee with a fork."

As for Steve himself, he had no complaints about pitching for the Phils, despite their lowly standing in the cellar. It just didn't seem like a last-place team when he was out there.

"There's no magic when I pitch," he said. "The club just seems to play good ball behind me. It's as if they know they're going to be in the ballgame and play accordingly. I've got no complaints about the support I've been getting."

When Steve won his 15th straight and 20th of the year, he set a team record for consecutive wins. Then he finally lost one. But it took the Atlanta Braves 11 innings and some strong pitching of their own to beat him, 2–1. And while his team was hopelessly buried in the basement, Steve didn't let up right until the final day of the year.

In fact, he was even stronger down the stretch. After losing a few more tough ones, he buckled down and gave up just four runs in his final five starts, pitching 44 innings. And when he was an 11–1 winner in the final game of the year, he had completed perhaps the most incredible pitching season in baseball history.

Steve Carlton finished with a 27–10 record, tying him with the great Sandy Koufax for most wins by a National League lefthander in a single season. Even more impressive was the fact that the Phils as a team won just 59 games. So Lefty had won an amazing 45.8 percent of his team's victories. The club was 59–97 with his totals, and only 32–87 without them. That's how good Steve Carlton's season was, and how bad the rest of the team had been.

His remaining stats testify to this most incredible season. Steve led the National League in starts with 41 and in complete games with 30. His 346.1 innings were also the best in the league, as were his 310 strikeouts. He tossed eight shutouts and had a league-leading 1.97

earned run average. Needless to say, he won the Cy Young Award as the best pitcher in the league.

If Steve Carlton had pitched with a pennant winner in 1972, his season still would have been a very great one. But given the fact that he was pitching for a last-place team, a team that lost almost 100 games, the season that Steve Carlton put together has to be considered one of the greatest ever.

A Perfect Moment . . . Almost

The most difficult feat for a pitcher to perform is to hurl a perfect game. That is, twenty-seven batters up, and twenty-seven batters down. No one reaches base via anything—hits, walks, even errors. Not surprisingly, the perfect game is a rarity, and whenever one is pitched, it's a great moment to be savored.

But there was one great moment involving a perfect game that wasn't quite savored in the same way as the others. It's been called by many the greatest pitching performance of all time, yet the disappointment when the game ended had to be overwhelming.

Confused? That's understandable. After all, how could one of the greatest pitching performances of all time be an overwhelming disappointment? It's simple. The performance resulted in that rarest of baseball rarities, the perfect game. The problem was—the pitcher lost!

It happened on May 26, 1959. The pitcher was Pittsburgh's Harvey Haddix, a little southpaw who was en route to a mediocre 12–12 season. Haddix would win 136 games in a career that lasted fourteen years, but would forever be remembered for a game he lost. But what a game it was. For on that cool spring night in

Milwaukee, Harvey Haddix had the good stuff, as good as any pitcher ever had.

The Pirates were playing a strong Braves team, defending National League champs, and they were pitching their ace righthander, Lew Burdette, who had personally destroyed the New York Yankees in the World Series of 1957 by starting and winning three games. Burdette was a crafty performer often accused of throwing an illegal spitball when he got in trouble. In 1959 he would win 21 games for the Braves and was a more than formidable opponent for Haddix and the Bucs.

As the early innings passed quickly, Milwaukee fans settled back for what looked like a pitchers' battle. Neither team had scored, though the Pirates threatened several times against Burdette. But the veteran got out of trouble each time.

Then somewhere around the fifth or sixth inning the fans began to realize that something special might be unfolding before them. Harvey Haddix had yet to allow a baserunner. He was retiring the Braves, one-two-three, one-two-three, one-two-three. Soon, the tension began mounting. Could Harvey Haddix pitch a perfect game?

But along with that came still another thought. What if the Pirates didn't score? What if Haddix was still perfect through nine and the game scoreless? That had never happened before in the long history of the game.

Sure enough, when the Pirates came to bat in the ninth, they still hadn't scored a run. Once again, Lew Burdette set them down. They had managed nine singles thus far, but each time they threatened to score, the veteran Burdette shut the door. Now Harvey Haddix had to take the mound to face the Braves in the bottom of the ninth.

What could the little lefty have been thinking as he took his warm-ups? Three more outs and he'd have a perfect game, twenty-seven Braves set down in order. But even if he did it, he wouldn't be able to celebrate. In fact, he had to get the three outs just to bring the game into extra innings.

Once more Haddix retired the Braves in order, and now even the partisan Milwaukee fans let out a huge roar. They had witnessed a perfect game. Or had they? Since the game had to continue, very few knew what the ruling would be regarding Haddix's performance thus far. And by this time the wire services had picked up the story. Now baseball fans across the country were following the action in Milwaukee.

In the tenth, the Pirates went down again, and out came Haddix once more. One-two-three. Same thing in the eleventh. Then the twelfth. One-two-three. One-two-three. Harvey Haddix had been perfect through 12 innings. Thirty-six Braves had come to bat and thirty-six had been retired. Yet the game still had to continue. The Pirates just could not score against Lew Burdette.

Then in the top of the 13th, Burdette set the Pirates down again. He had now given up 12 hits, all singles, but he stubbornly refused to allow a run. Haddix, of course, had allowed nothing. He had already produced the greatest single pitching performance in baseball history. But he couldn't relax, couldn't savor it. He had to return to the mound for the 13th time. It couldn't go on forever.

Second baseman Felix Mantilla led off the 13th. Haddix worked him carefully and got him to hit a

Pittsburgh lefthander Harvey Haddix in action during his 12-inning masterpiece against the 1959 Milwaukee Braves. Haddix made baseball history by retiring 36 straight batters, a 12-inning perfect game—that Pittsburgh lost! In the 13th inning, the Braves finally scored one run and won the game.

routine bouncer to third. Don Hoak picked it up . . . and threw it away! An error. The perfect string had been broken after thirty-six batters. Haddix just hung his head for a minute, letting all the pent-up emotion drain from him. Then he took a deep breath. The outcome of the game was still at stake.

A sacrifice bunt moved Mantilla to second. Then Haddix walked Hank Aaron intentionally to set up a possible double play. The next batter was the ever-dangerous Joe Adcock, and while he tried to work the big slugger carefully, Haddix's luck had finally run out.

Adcock tagged one, a long drive to deep right-center that just fell over the fence for an apparent three-run homer. The game was over. After pitching 12 perfect innings, Harvey Haddix would have nothing more than a loss on his pitching record.

In a final irony, Hank Aaron, thinking the ball hit the base of the fence, touched second, saw Mantilla score, and then headed for the dugout. Adcock was ruled out when he went to third and technically passed Aaron on the bases. So the only hit against Harvey Haddix was officially scored a double and the Braves had won it 1–0, instead of 3–0.

To ease the pain somewhat, Haddix was officially given credit for a 12-inning perfect game. But being a competitor, he undoubtedly saw it as a heartbreaking loss instead of a piece of brilliant baseball history, at least when it happened.

Looking back now, Haddix's masterpiece is viewed as perhaps the single most dramatic and impressive pitching performance in baseball history. And no one, not Lew Burdette, not Joe Adcock, nor the final outcome of the game, can erase the magnitude of that great moment. For 12 innings, Harvey Haddix was perfect. No one, before or since, has ever been that good.

A Historic Moment, and a
Great Ballplayer, Too

The years have passed before us and several genera-
tions of new baseball fans have come on the scene
since Jackie Robinson first donned the uniform of the
Brooklyn Dodgers in 1947. Looking back, it's hard to
believe that so much time has gone by since a moment
occurred that may have been the most historically sig-
nificant in all of baseball. Yet at the same time, it's also
difficult to believe that no black man had ever played
major league baseball up to 1947.

This will be an especially difficult concept for the
younger fans used to watching dominant black players
ever since they can remember. From the days of Jackie
Robinson, through Willie Mays and Hank Aaron, Bob
Gibson and Frank Robinson, to Rickey Henderson and
Dwight Gooden today, black players have provided
scores of thrills, record-breaking performances, and
great moments. Yet before 1947 there simply were no
black players in the major leagues.

There was never a written edict that kept blacks out
of the majors, just an unwritten "color line" that no
one in baseball allowed to be crossed until a daring,
innovative executive named Branch Rickey came

along. Rickey was running the Brooklyn Dodger organization in the 1940s, and he was not only the one who decided it was time for blacks to play big league baseball, he was also the one who did something about it.

But what of all the fine black ballplayers who came before? Surely there were those fully capable of playing in the majors and performing as brilliantly as those playing today. That goes without saying. Only these players had to settle for the segregated Negro Leagues, which for the most part consisted of loosely organized groups of barnstorming teams playing before black fans in any available ballpark, field, or cow pasture.

Very few of these ballplayers made nearly the money the big leaguers received during the same period, though certainly a large number of them would have been able to compete at the major league level if given the chance. And several of these Negro League stars, such as pitcher Satchel Paige and catcher Josh Gibson, were so good that there is little doubt they could have been superstars in the majors.

But what of Jackie Robinson? What was the road he took that led to his being the first black man to pull on the uniform of a major league team? The road wasn't easy. It may have been paved with athletic success, but it was also blocked often by the ugly appearance of racial prejudice.

Jack Roosevelt Robinson was born on January 31, 1919, at Cairo, Georgia. He was the last of five children born to Jerry and Mallie Robinson. His family were farmers, though they had always worked someone else's land. When Jackie was just six months old, his father left home to seek a better life. He said he was going to see his brother in Texas. But he never went to

Texas and didn't return, either. Finally, Mallie Robinson packed her family up and left.

She tried to find some odd jobs in the area, but it was difficult. It also wasn't easy for a black family living in Georgia back then, so Mallie Robinson heeded the advice of her brother and took her family to California. They settled into a small apartment in Los Angeles, and that's where Jackie grew up. Life was never easy, but Mallie Robinson was a strong woman and she held her family together.

Jackie took to sports early. In fact, when he was just in elementary school, he told his mother she could stop making him lunches every day. When she asked why, he explained that he was the best ballplayer in the class and other kids were always giving him part of their lunches so he would play on their team.

Unfortunately, he also learned that things would never be easy because of the color of his skin. Jackie himself recalled that when he was about eight years old, a little girl came by and began calling him, "Nigger, nigger, nigger!" But as would always be his way, Jackie fought back, and ended up in a stone-throwing bout with the girl's father.

There were enough good influences to keep him out of real trouble, and pretty soon sports dominated his life. He began to rack up an impressive set of athletic credentials. At Muir Technical High School Jackie was a star in football, basketball, and baseball. From there, he went to Pasadena Junior College, where he added track to his repertoire.

His first year there he broke his brother Mack's school broad-jump record, leaping 25 feet, 6½ inches. In baseball, he hit .417 and swiped 25 bases in 24 games and led his team to the championship. In the stands that spring day in 1938 was veteran baseball man Jimmy Dykes, who approached Jackie's coach after the game and said: "That Robinson kid could play major league baseball at a moment's notice."

Well, the moment's notice was still nine years away, and Jackie Robinson wasn't one to stand on his laurels. After another great football season at Pasadena, he transferred to UCLA, where he immediately became a running sensation, so good that Stanford coach Claude Thornhill called him "the greatest backfield runner I've seen in all my connection with football—and that goes back some twenty-five years."

Jackie led the nation in 1939 by averaging more than twelve yards a carry from scrimmage and twenty-one yards a pop on punt returns. He was also a basketball and baseball star there, and perhaps even more importantly, he met his future wife, Rachel Isum, who would remain steadfastly by his side during the tough times that would follow.

But Jackie also began to make some hard decisions at this time. He left UCLA after two years and within sight of graduation because he had come to believe "that no amount of education would help a black man get a job. I was living in an academic and athletic dream world. It was time for me to help my mother and my family."

So Jackie went to work as an assistant athletic director at a work camp sponsored by the National Youth Administration. His job was to help underprivileged youngsters stay off the streets, learn a trade, and play sports as an outlet. Their goal was to shape a better future for these kids. Jackie enjoyed the work, but soon after, in December of 1941, the Japanese bombed Pearl Harbor and the United States became embroiled in World War II.

Jackie entered the army and again found racial prejudice everywhere. Yet he fought to be admitted to Officers' Candidate School and made it. Once he graduated, he fought to get equal rights for black enlisted men. Later, there was an incident on a bus that actually resulted in court-martial charges being brought against him, but Jackie was exonerated and later applied for a discharge. With the war winding down, he got it and, in late 1944, became basketball coach at Sam Houston College, a small black school in Texas.

He enjoyed coaching and whipped a good team into shape quickly. But his coaching career didn't last long. In April of 1945, he had an offer to play baseball for the Kansas City Monarchs, one of the top teams in the Negro League. Jackie and the Monarchs agreed on a contract that would pay him $400 a month. He was now a professional baseball player, but he still gave no thoughts to competing in the major leagues.

Life with the Monarchs wasn't easy. There were long bus rides, bad food, poor living conditions, playing fields that were less than first rate. Only the competition was good. Yet even that was often overshadowed by the constant threat of racial prejudice, which could sometimes take a violent turn. But Jackie and many of the others were professionals, even if it was in a totally segregated league.

At about the same time Jackie was playing and starring for the Monarchs, events were taking place in Brooklyn that would ultimately change Jackie's life as well as the face of baseball forever. Branch Rickey of the Dodgers began scouting black players in earnest. He told people he was thinking about starting another Negro League, but in reality he had something much more daring in mind.

In the spring of 1945, Jackie and two other black players were called to Boston, allegedly to try out for the Red Sox. The tryout was held because a Boston councilman had threatened to pass a law against Sunday baseball if the Sox didn't integrate the team. But the tryout was merely a smokescreen.

"I laughed a little every time I caught a ball during that tryout," Jackie recalled later. "I knew we were just going through the motions."

The Red Sox didn't sign a black then, but a short time later Branch Rickey asked black sportswriter Wendell Smith if any of the three players were good enough to make the majors.

"Yeah, Jackie Robinson," Smith said without hesitation. "He could make good in any league."

That's when Branch Rickey really began to look at Jackie Robinson in earnest. He knew he needed a special man for what he was about to do. Rickey called it his "noble experiment," and he was searching for someone with all the necessary qualities. He eliminated such fine ballplayers as Don Newcombe and Roy Campanella, both of whom would become Dodger stars a few years later. But with all Rickey's scouting and investigating, Jackie stayed on the top of the list.

Finally, the two men met on August 28, 1945. Jackie didn't even know exactly why Branch Rickey wanted to see him. He thought it might be to talk about the rumored new Negro League. But then Branch Rickey came to the point.

"Jackie, you were brought here to play for the Brooklyn organization, perhaps starting out in Montreal."

Jackie couldn't believe his ears. Montreal was the home of the Dodgers' top farm club. But when Branch Rickey laid it all out for him, Jackie Robinson knew that his might be the toughest debut any baseball player ever had. As Rickey said, "There's virtually nobody on our side. No owners, no umpires, very few newspapermen. And I'm afraid the fans may be hostile. We'll be in a tough position. We can win only if we can convince the world that I'm doing this because you're a great ballplayer and a fine gentleman."

Rickey then began to create situations that might occur, baseball situations where the white players would more than likely insult Jackie with every kind of racial slur they could remember. They might also go out of their way to be physically rougher with him than was necessary. He kept asking Jackie what he would do. Finally, Jackie asked:

"Mr. Rickey, do you want a ballplayer who's afraid to fight back?"

"I want a ballplayer with guts enough not to fight back!" Rickey said quickly.

He then explained that at first Jackie couldn't fight back. "This is a battle in which you'll have to swallow an awful lot of pride and count on base hits and stolen bases to do the job."

After more than three hours, Rickey was sure that Jackie Robinson was the right man and he offered him a bonus of $3,500 and a salary of $600 a month to play with the Montreal Royals. Like the Dodgers, the Royals had never had a black in uniform before. Even

Jackie Robinson became the first black man to play in the majors when he joined the Brooklyn Dodgers in 1947. Despite playing under tremendous pressure, he excelled at bat, in the field, and on the bases, where he drove opposing pitchers crazy. Here, he dives safely back to first, slipping under the glove of Cincinnati first baseman Ted Kluszewski.

though he knew it would be the toughest thing he ever did, Jackie accepted on the spot.

Jackie's signing really caused an uproar. Many thought it was wrong, that blacks shouldn't be allowed to play. Others questioned whether Jackie was good enough to make it. Even people who had been saying that blacks should be allowed questioned whether the time was right. But the historic moment was fast approaching.

Jackie was married in February, 1946, and he and Rachel went to Florida for spring training with Montreal. There was a great deal of prejudice in Florida. Jackie and Rachel had to live with local black families and he could rarely eat with the rest of the team. Contrary to legend, there was a second black with Montreal that year, a pitcher named John Wright. He, too, was signed by Rickey, but without the kind of indoctrination Jackie had. Wright wasn't really as talented a player and didn't last out the season.

But Jackie Robinson did. Once he got rid of an early season case of jitters, he began playing great ball as Montreal's second baseman. Despite many racial incidents, he prevailed, leading the International League with a .349 batting average, driving home 66 runs, and also leading the league in stolen bases.

Jackie had proven many things to many people. He had been put in the pressure cooker and produced. In fact, toward the end of the 1946 season, one sports columnist wrote that players like Ted Williams, Bob Feller, Dixie Walker, and Hal Newhouser were having great years in the majors, but added, "The greatest performance being put on anywhere in sport . . . is being supplied by . . . Jackie Robinson of Montreal, who is playing baseball under pressures that would have crushed a less courageous man."

The next question was logical. Where would Jackie be playing in 1947? He was still on the Montreal roster, but there were those who felt it was just temporary. Branch Rickey didn't want to cause any furor ahead of time. In addition, he had already signed Don Newcombe and Roy Campanella to Montreal contracts, so he was obviously continuing his plan to sign black ballplayers. But the historical moment would belong to Jackie Robinson.

Sure enough, shortly before the season was to start, it was announced that Brooklyn had purchased Jackie's contract from Montreal. He was officially a Dodger. Because the Dodgers had an established second baseman in Eddie Stanky, Jackie would be playing an unfamiliar position, first base. But he agreed to do it.

Once again, Branch Rickey warned him that the pressure would be tremendous, that he had to turn the other cheek no matter what was said to him. Once again he would have to answer with base hits, stolen bases, and RBIs.

There was even talk of a petition circulating among some members of the Dodgers asking Rickey not to make Jackie a member of the team. But Rickey wouldn't hear of it. Anyone who felt he couldn't play alongside a black man would be traded. Fortunately, the team's young stars, like Pee Wee Reese and Gil Hodges, accepted Jackie immediately.

The historic moment came on April 15, 1947. Jackie Robinson was the starting first baseman for the Brooklyn Dodgers, the first black man to appear in a major league ballgame in the twentieth century. He was hitless that day, but his sacrifice bunt caused an error that led to the winning run as the Dodgers beat the Boston Braves.

So a black man had played and baseball didn't fold up. Jackie got off to a slow start, going hitless in his first twenty at bats. But then in a game against the Phillies, Jackie was taking a terrible baiting from some of the Phils. Still following Rickey's orders, he kept his mouth shut. Suddenly Eddie Stanky barked at the Phils: "Listen, you yellow-bellied cowards, why don't you yell at somebody who can answer back?"

And at the same time shortstop Reese walked over and put his arm around Jackie's shoulder in a sign of solidarity. That gesture seemed to relax Jackie as well as the team. After that, he began playing the kind of ball Branch Rickey felt he was capable of all along. He finished his rookie year with a .297 batting average, 12

From the great Brooklyn Dodgers teams of the late 1940s and early 1950s, (left to right) Gil Hodges, Junior Gilliam, Pee Wee Reese, and Jackie Robinson.

homers, and 48 RBIs. All this despite a constant barrage of hate mail, death threats, and all the racial name-calling anyone can imagine. It took a real strong man to persevere. And to top it all, the Dodgers won the pennant.

Jackie Robinson was twenty-eight years old when he broke the color line in 1947. If there had been no color line, he undoubtedly would have had a much longer career. A year later Stanky was traded, Gil Hodges took over at first, and Jackie moved to second. The Dodgers would win the National League pennant in five of Jackie's remaining nine years.

When he finally retired after the 1956 season, he had a .311 lifetime batting average and more than 1,500 hits. He also had a National League Most Valuable Player award for his 1949 season, which saw him bat .342, with 16 homers and 124 runs batted in. But this is not a story of statistics, it's about a courageous man who paved the way for many others to follow.

In his later years, Jackie Robinson often took a stand when he saw evidence of racial injustice. To some, he was a troublemaker and an agitator. But he was just a man who spoke up when he felt it was necessary. One of the last causes he championed again involved baseball. Jackie felt it was time for a black manager, that with so many black players in the early 1970s, a black manager was long overdue.

He never lived to see that happen. Jackie Robinson died of a heart attack on October 24, 1972, at the age of fifty-three. Some felt that the pressures and incredible tension he endured in becoming the first black player contributed to his declining health and early death.

And when Frank Robinson (no relation to Jackie) was named the majors' first black manager in the fall of 1974, he closed his press conference with these words: "If I had one wish in the world today," he said, "it would be that Jackie Robinson could be here to see this happen."

There were many in the audience who felt the same way.

World Series Perfect

This one wasn't anticipated by anyone. Sure, there was a possibility that it could happen someday, but in more than half a century of World Series play, it hadn't. And the man who finally did it was just as unlikely as the event itself. If anyone was going to pitch a no-hitter, let alone a perfect game, in World Series play, it would be one of the game's superstars. Right? Wrong. It was a journeyman pitcher who retired with a losing record for his career.

It happened back in 1956. The New York Yankees were playing the Brooklyn Dodgers in another of their so-called subway series. The two teams, in fact, were meeting in the series for the sixth time in ten years. Their matchups were usually classics, even though the Yanks won each time, with the exception of 1955. But that didn't make the rivalry any less heated.

These were the Dodgers of "Boys of Summer" fame. There was Pee Wee Reese, Gil Hodges, Roy Campanella, Duke Snider, Carl Furillo, Don Newcombe, Carl Erskine, and Jackie Robinson, as well as a talented supporting cast. As for the Bronx Bombers, well, they were in the midst of another dynasty, having won five straight pennants and World Series from 1949 to 1953. After yielding to the Cleveland Indians in 1954, they were off on another run of pennants from 1955 to 1958.

The Yanks were also made up of stars and superstars. There was Mickey Mantle and Yogi Berra, Gil McDougald and "Moose" Skowron, Hank Bauer and Billy Martin, Whitey Ford and Bob Turley. And, as usual, the team had a mixture of veterans and role players who made the roster powerful from top to bottom.

In the opener at Ebbets Field in Brooklyn, the Yanks sent their ace, Whitey Ford, against veteran Sal Maglie. Maglie had been the ace of the New York Giants pitching staff in the early 1950s, but at age thirty-nine he was considered finished. Coming to the Dodgers from Cleveland early in the season, he had a last hurrah with a 13–5 record. He proved it was no fluke in the Series, upsetting Ford and the Yanks, 6–3.

Game two provided a mild surprise. Brooklyn started its 27-game winner, Don Newcombe, while the Yanks countered with Don Larsen, who had compiled an 11–5 mark while doubling as a reliever and spot starter during the regular season. Larsen was a curious choice for several reasons.

A 6'4", 230-pounder, Larsen seemed to have all the ingredients to be a big winner. But he wasn't. In fact, when he started his career with the old St. Louis Browns in 1953, he had a 7–12 record. A year later, when the team moved to Baltimore, Larsen had the worst record in the majors, finishing a dismal 3–21.

Nevertheless, the Yanks traded for Larsen and he was 9–2 for the Bombers in 1955. But some felt it was only because he had the Yankee bats behind him, and when he got a start in the World Series that year, he was belted out in just four innings. And while he managed an 11–5 mark in '56, most Yankee fans felt a bit leery when he took the mound in game two.

Once again it looked as if the big bats of the Bronx Bombers would make Larsen a winner. They gave the big righthander a 6–0 lead in the second inning. But Larsen couldn't hold it. The Dodgers came back with six runs of their own in the second, driving a wild Larsen (he had given up four walks) from the mound. From there, the Dodgers went on to a 13–8 victory and 2–0 lead in the Series.

But when the scene shifted to Yankee Stadium, things changed. With Whitey Ford again pitching, the Yanks won game three, 5–3. Then knuckleballer Tom Sturdivant tamed the Dodgers, 6–2, in game four. The Series was squared at two games each, setting the stage for the pivotal fifth game. Maglie would return to the mound for the Dodgers, and most people figured the Yanks would counter with 18-game winner Johnny Kucks.

That's when Yanks manager Casey Stengel surprised everyone. He once again tabbed Don Larsen as his starting pitcher. Was this one of the Ol' Perfesser's hunches? There was no logical reason for the choice. And the more than 64,000 fans who jammed into Yankee Stadium on Monday, October 8, 1956, couldn't have realized they were about to see baseball history in the making.

Both pitchers had one-two-three innings in the first. Then Jackie Robinson, leading off the Dodger second, hit a shot right at New York third baseman Andy

52

Carey. The ball bounced off Carey's glove, but caroomed right to shortstop McDougald, who fired to first to nip Robinson by half a step.

It was the closest thing to a hit either team would get in the first three innings. By the time the Dodgers came up in the top of the fourth, neither pitcher had yielded a thing. Eighteen batters had come up, and eighteen had gone down. Something had to give. But in the fourth, Larsen again set the Dodgers down in order. It was beginning to look as if Stengel's hunch was a good one. The big guy certainly seemed to have his good stuff.

But so did Maglie. Sal the Barber, as he was called, began the bottom of the fourth by retiring Bauer and Joe Collins. Now Mickey Mantle was up, batting left-handed against the veteran righty. With two strikes on him, the Mick drove a Maglie curveball down the right-field line and into the lower stands for a home run. The huge crowd went wild as the young slugger circled the bases. It was the first hit of the game for either side and it gave the Yanks a 1–0 lead.

Then came the Dodger fifth and the question that began creeping into everyone's mind. How long could Larsen's magic continue? The big righty got Jackie Robinson to start the inning. Now first baseman Gil Hodges was at the plate, wig-wagging his bat menacingly at Larsen. The pitcher delivered and Hodges swung. Momentarily, some 64,000 fans held their collective breaths.

The powerful first sacker sent a long drive into deep left-center, known as Death Valley at Yankee Stadium. At first it looked as if it would go between the outfielders for at least a double or triple. But centerfielder

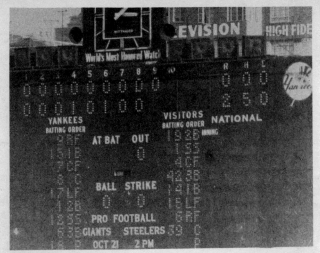

The scoreboard tells the tale after Larsen's perfect
World Series game—for the Dodgers it's no runs, no
hits, no errors!

Mantle turned on his great speed and made a marvelous backhanded catch in the left-centerfield
gap.

Next came leftfielder Sandy Amoros. A lefthanded
batter, Amoros jumped on a fastball and sent a deep
drive down the rightfield line. It sailed into the lower
stands for . . . a foul strike! The ball was foul by just
inches. With a reprieve, Larsen then got Amoros to
ground out to second, retiring the side once more . . .
in order.

The sixth inning was easier. Furillo, Campanella, and
Maglie went out without a whimper. Eighteen Dodgers
up; eighteen Dodgers down. Now, just about everyone
knew what was happening. In the dugout, the other
Yankees began ignoring Larsen. There is an old base-

54

ball superstition that you didn't mention a no-hitter in progress. If you do, you might jinx the pitcher.

Even Larsen himself had to look at the scoreboard to be reminded of what he was doing. And he later said that when he realized he had a no-hitter going, he still didn't think it was a perfect game.

"I thought I had walked a man or two somewhere along the line."

No-hitters, of course, are rare; perfect games even more elusive. But in the World Series, neither had ever been done. Perhaps the closest call came just nine years before, in the 1947 Series, also between the Dodgers and Yanks. It happened in the fourth game when the Yankees' Floyd Bevens entered the ninth inning with a no-hit game in the works, but he ended up giving up a walk and a hit, and lost the game 3–2.

That was the closest anyone had come to World Series immortality, but as Don Larsen lumbered out to the mound for the seventh inning, he had a chance to produce a great moment of his own.

He even had a bit more of a cushion, getting a second run in the sixth on a single by Carey, his own sacrifice bunt, and an RBI base hit by Hank Bauer. So it was 2–0 as Larsen went back to work, this time nailing the top of the Dodger order, Gilliam, Reese, and Snider for the third time. He was now six outs away.

The tension built with each pitch as Larsen started working the eighth. First Jackie Robinson went down, then Gil Hodges, and finally Sandy Amoros. As Larsen came back to the dugout for the final time, the huge Stadium crowd was in a frenzy. His teammates still gave him the silent treatment—he was only three outs from a perfect game.

The dangerous Carl Furillo was first up, the same Furillo who had started the rally against Bevens nine years before. After fouling off four pitches, Furillo flied to right and Hank Bauer was there to make the catch. One out. Now came Roy Campanella, another dangerous hitter. After fouling off the first pitch, Campy hit a weak grounder to short. McDougald threw him out easily. The crowd went wild again. One more batter left.

Maglie was due up. The veteran righthander had pitched valiantly, but it was obvious he wouldn't be batting. Instead, Manager Walter Alston sent up Dale Mitchell, a solid lefthanded hitter, who had come to the Dodgers in a midseason trade with Cleveland. Mitchell was a good contact hitter and his job was to get wood on the ball and try to get something started. After all, the Dodgers weren't thinking about Larsen's gem. They were only trailing 2–0, and still wanted to win the game.

Larsen stared in and fired a fastball. It was off the plate for a ball. Catcher Berra saw that Larsen still had good velocity and decided that, with all the tension, fastballs were the best bet. He called for another one and it cut the plate for a strike. Again the big guy fired a hard one and this time Mitchell swung . . . and missed! Strike two.

The fans at the big ballpark were on their feet. Countless others were glued to their radios and televisions as Larsen set to throw again. Another fastball. Protecting the plate, Mitchell swung and fouled it off. Still a 1–2 count. Still the tension, still baseball history riding with each pitch. Once more Larsen peered in

Yankee catcher Yogi Berra (8) leaps into the arms of pitcher Don Larsen after the big righthander completed the only perfect game in World Series history. Larsen shut out the Brooklyn Dodgers 2–0 in the fifth game of the 1956 Fall Classic, retiring all the batters he faced.

toward the plate. Using his no-windup style of delivery, he fired again.

This time Mitchell started to offer, but held up. The ball caught the outside corner of the plate. Umpire Babe Pinelli threw up his right hand and a roar went up from the huge crowd. It was called strike three! Larsen had done it. He had pitched a no-hitter and perfect game in the World Series, the first and only man to do it.

As he ran triumphantly from the mound, catcher Berra ran out and leaped at his pitcher in jubilation. In a classic picture, fans everywhere saw Yogi hanging on to his big pitcher's neck with Larsen holding Yogi off the ground. And why not celebrate? It was one of baseball's all-time greatest moments.

An Unplanned Farewell

There are many kinds of great moments, but this one was perhaps the saddest. In fact, it wasn't even recognized for what it was until months later, when a tragedy robbed the game of baseball of one of its greatest players. And it came at a time when that player was just getting long overdue recognition as one of the greats of his time.

The player was Roberto Clemente, the strong-armed outfielder of the Pittsburgh Pirates. Clemente had come to the Pirates as a twenty-year-old rookie in 1955. By the time the 1972 season rolled around, the same Roberto Clemente was just 118 hits short of joining the exclusive 3,000 hit club—a sure sign of a great career.

Yet it was also a career that saw recognition come belatedly, and a career not without controversy. Clemente could do it all on a ballfield. He was not only a great hitter, but a great defensive player as well, with a throwing arm second to none. He won the National League batting title four times, and seemed to get better with age.

If there was one drawback, it was that Roberto didn't hit a whole lot of home runs. Oh, he had power, but swinging for the fences wasn't his style. And in the homer-happy 1960s, this trait prevented him from getting the full credit he deserved. He was often rated a notch below the three ranking superstars of the era—Henry Aaron, Willie Mays, and Mickey Mantle. The reason was simple. They hit more round-trippers.

But in truth, Clemente was every bit the ballplayer they were, and he finally got a chance to prove it when the Pirates made it into the 1971 World Series. Roberto was thirty-seven years old then, but coming off another fine season in which he batted .341.

In the Series that year, the Pirates defeated the Baltimore Orioles in seven games. Roberto Clemente batted .414 in the Fall Classic, banging out 12 hits in twenty-nine trips. Among them were two doubles, a triple, a pair of homers, and four RBIs. In addition, he made several brilliant plays in rightfield, showing he had lost none of his speed and displaying the throwing arm that had been the scourge of National League runners for years. And in the deciding seventh game he homered in the fourth inning to give the Pirates a 1–0 lead in a game they eventually won, 2–1.

Fittingly, Roberto was named the Most Valuable Player in the Series and was now within 118 hits of the magical 3,000 mark, which would put him in company with baseball's best. It was a foregone conclusion that he would get those needed hits in 1972.

Roberto was a native of Puerto Rico, having been born in Carolina, Puerto Rico, on August 18, 1934. He was originally signed into the Brooklyn Dodger organization, but the Pirates drafted him from the Dodgers in 1953 and elevated him to the majors two years later. The Pirates, at the time, were one of baseball's poorer teams, but maybe that was good, because it got Roberto to the majors sooner.

He hit just .255 his rookie year and in his first five seasons hit .300 only once. But after that, he hit below .300 just one time. The Pirates won the pennant in 1960 with Roberto hitting .314. He was also a .310 hitter in the World Series against the Yankees that year, but he still got very little recognition. He was beginning to get angry and the next year hit .351 to take his first batting title.

Many people in those days envisioned Roberto as an angry man. He was often outspoken, said what was on his mind, and didn't appreciate the fact that he wasn't rated as highly as the other superstars of the day.

"I play baseball the way it is supposed to be played," he once said. "I do not think there is anyone who does all the things as well. I think I am the best."

His pride and competitive fires drove Roberto to play very hard. On those occasions when he was injured, it seemed there was always someone to say he was dogging it. That was another bum rap that finally disappeared in his later years. He had his best power year in 1966, hitting 29 homers and driving home 119 runs. He was the National League's Most Valuable Player that year, but his batting average was just .317. He really preferred to hit to all fields and not worry about homers.

The next year he proved it by hitting a solid .357, and two years later, at age thirty-five, he hit .345. The next year it was .352. He seemed to be getting better with age, and the recognition was starting to come. Then came the pennant-winning year of 1971 and a .341 average. By then, Mantle had already retired and Mays was nearing the end of the line. More and more people began to see Roberto Clemente as the true superstar he had always been.

Then came 1972, the year everyone figured he would get 3,000 hits. By that time, he also had another goal which had become every bit as important as his baseball achievements. He wanted to raise enough money to start a giant sports city in his native Puerto Rico, a place kids could go and learn about sports and about being good citizens at the same time. He said that was one reason he continued to play.

"If they gave me the money to start my sports city right now, I would retire," he said. "Otherwise, I still play a few more years."

But 1972 turned out to be a difficult year for Roberto. A series of nagging injuries would limit him to just 102 games. No longer were the 118 hits he needed to reach 3,000 a cinch. He was still hitting over .300, but the injuries were taking their toll. What it came down to was this. The Pirates were meeting the New York Mets in the final game of the regular season. Roberto had 117 hits for the year, 2,999 for his career. He needed one more.

To most people, this was no big deal. After all, Roberto had already announced that he intended to play again in 1973. If he didn't get the final hit, he'd simply get it the next year. There were obviously still a lot of hits left in his quick bat.

So when Roberto stepped to the plate to face Mets' Jon Matlack in the fourth inning, the 13,117 fans at Three Rivers Stadium didn't stir much. Roberto wig-wagged his bat in familiar fashion, then jumped on a Matlack fastball and lashed a solid double for his

This is the view the pitcher had when he faced the immortal Roberto Clemente. Clemente earned his 3,000th hit in his last at-bat of the 1972 season, only a few months before his tragic death.

3,000th hit, becoming the eleventh player in baseball history to reach that milestone. It was a typical Clemente hit in that it ignited a three-run Pirate rally that enabled the Bucs to win the game, 5–0.

The announcement of Roberto's 3,000th hit brought a standing ovation from the sparse crowd, but no one realized at the time what a historic moment they had just witnessed.

In late December of 1972, a terrible earthquake leveled the Latin American city of Managua, Nicaragua. Many thousands were killed, and countless thousands injured and homeless. Food was scarce. There was little clean water. It was a disaster of major proportions.

Being the kind of person he was, Roberto Clemente acted quickly. He wanted the Puerto Rican people to help the victims in Nicaragua and quickly organized a drive to gather food and clothing. The drive was a huge success, and on the night of December 31, 1972, Roberto made plans to take the aid to Managua.

Shortly after nine o'clock, Roberto boarded a four-engine DC-7 with four other men, ready to fly the supplies to the quake victims. Roberto's wife didn't want him to go. She felt the plane was old and overloaded, but he assured her everything would be all right, that he would be back to celebrate the New Year and to meet Pirate general manager Joe Brown, who was flying to Puerto Rico with Roberto's 1973 contract.

The plane took off from San Juan International Airport, and within minutes developed engine problems. It came down in heavy seas just a mile and a half from shore, but before rescuers could reach the scene, the plane and all aboard were lost. It was a terrible tragedy for the Clemente family, for Puerto Rico, for Managua, and for baseball.

It was Roberto's tragic death that reminded people just how important that final hit had been. Not that it really mattered in the overall context of Roberto Clemente's life and tragic death. But in the statistical-conscious world of baseball, it elevated him to the place where he belonged, with the elite of the game. Because Hall of Famer Roberto Clemente was a great man as well as a great player, and his many great moments simply serve to prove it all over again.

An Unlikely Hero, an Unlikely Moment

In 1977, the New York Yankees returned to the prominence of earlier years by winning the American League pennant, then taking the World Series from the Los Angeles Dodgers in six games. The Yanks' newest slugger, veteran Reggie Jackson, who was obtained as a free agent, upheld the tradition of such former Bombers as Babe Ruth, Lou Gehrig, Joe DiMaggio, and Mickey Mantle, when he blasted three home runs in the final game to lock up the New York victory.

So when 1978 rolled around, most experts picked the Yanks to repeat as American League kingpins and reach the Fall Classic once more. The Yanks had a talented and deep team. But there was a problem. Perhaps it was too many egos. The team always seemed to be bickering, nit-picking, or actually fighting. There were volatile players like Reggie, Thurman Munson, Graig Nettles, and Lou Piniella. The manager was Billy Martin, brash, outspoken, and prone to temper tantrums. And the owner was the equally flamboyant George Steinbrenner, who loved to be the center of attention, and also exhibited little patience with his players when they weren't playing well.

All of this pointed to trouble, especially if the team got off to a slow start. It wasn't so much a slow start, but a hot start by other teams in the usually red-hot, closely contested American League East. On May 18, for instance, the Yanks had a 19–13 record, but trailed Detroit at 21–9 and Boston at 23–12.

On May 24, the Red Sox went into first place, a position they would hold for the bulk of the season. Pretty soon, the internal squabbling began with the Yanks once more, as Boston continued to play well and increase its lead. By the All-Star Game break in July the Red Sox had a 57–26 record, the best in the majors, while the Yanks were struggling at 46–38, some 11½ games back and in third place.

It all reached a peak on July 18. The Red Sox increased their lead to 14 games over the bickering Yankees, who seemed all but out of it. But less than a week later, the Yanks made a change. They replaced the highly emotional Billy Martin with low-keyed Bob Lemon, and the new manager declared it was time to just let the players play ball.

Under Lemon, the Yankees seemed to relax and began playing great baseball. The Red Sox, at the same time, faltered, and their lead dropped. By the end of July it had been cut to seven and one-half games and the Yanks were still surging. On September 8, the red-hot Yankees came into Boston for a big, four-game series. They had cut the lead to a mere four games. Since the big 14-game lead in July, the Sox were 25–24, while the Yanks had a 35–14 log. Things had turned around so much that one observer put it this way: "This is the only time I can remember a first-place team chasing a second-place team."

67

Well, the Yanks not only swept the four-game series, they destroyed the Sox in the process, winning by scores of 15–3, 13–2, 7–0, and 7–4. They had scored 42 runs to just 9 for the Red Sox, getting 67 hits to 21 for their opponents. The faltering Sox also committed 12 errors in the four games. And more important, the sweep enabled the New Yorkers to draw even in the divisional race.

From there, it was a dogfight. The Yanks grabbed the lead, but the Red Sox wouldn't let them get too far in front. With six games left for each team, the Yankee lead was a single game. Red Sox star Carl Yastrzemski knew what his team had to do.

"We've got to win all six," Yaz said.

That's just what happened. But while the Sox were winning, so were the Yankees. Then the Bosox won their final and looked at the scoreboard to see what the New Yorkers were doing. They were in the process of getting bombed by Cleveland. So after 162 games, both clubs had identical 99–63 records. There would be a one-game playoff at Fenway Park in Boston to determine the divisional champion.

The Sox sent ex-Yankee Mike Torrez to the mound to face the Yanks' Ron Guidry. Guidry was in the midst of what is called a career season, having compiled a 24–3 record to that point. But when the Bosox's Carl Yastrzemski homered to make it 1–0 in the second, the feeling was that Guidry could be beaten. It stayed that way until the sixth when a Jim Rice single drove home the Sox's second run.

If the Yanks were going to pull it out, they would have to get something going soon. One of their stars, such as Jackson, Nettles, or Thurman Munson would have to come up with a big hit. With one out in the seventh, Chris Chambliss singled to left, and veteran Roy White slammed a base hit to center. After pinch hitter Jim Spencer flied out, the next hitter up was the Yanks' shortstop, Bucky Dent.

Many Yankee fans thought manager Lemon would pinch-hit for Dent, who was batting a shade over .240 and rarely hit a long ball. But the shortstop came up to face Torrez in what was certainly a clutch situation. The big righthander fired hard and Dent fouled the pitch off his foot. It was extremely painful, since it aggravated a foot injury Dent had sustained earlier in the year.

While Dent walked off the pain, he stopped to talk to leadoff man Mickey Rivers, who was in the on-deck circle. Suddenly, the two switched bats, and Dent came up again swinging Rivers' lumber. Maybe it was only a ballplayer's superstition, but it was about to pay huge dividends.

Torrez delivered again and Dent swung. The borrowed bat connected and the ball arched high and deep toward Fenway's short leftfield wall, known as the Green Monster. With Torrez, the Red Sox, and their loyal fans all watching, the ball cleared the wall for a dramatic, three-run home run, giving the Yanks a 3–2 lead. Light-hitting Bucky Dent had delivered one of the most dramatic home runs in Yankee history. It not only gave the New Yorkers the lead, but it seemed to take the heart out of the Red Sox.

A walk to Mickey Rivers finished Torrez. With Bob Stanley pitching, Mick the Quick stole second and scored on Thurm Munson's double, making it 4–2. Then in the top of the eighth, Mr. October, Reggie

69

Jackson took over, hitting a mammoth homer into the centerfield stands to make it a 5–2 game. The Sox closed to 5–4 in the eighth and gave the Yanks another scare in the ninth. But relief ace Rich Gossage hung on to close it out. The Yankees had won.

For the Red Sox, it was a bitter disappointment. The Yanks rejoiced, then went on to defeat the Kansas City Royals in the playoffs and the L.A. Dodgers once more in the World Series. It's all part of Yankee history now.

But the success of 1978 would never have happened had it not been for an unlikely hero. It was Bucky Dent who borrowed a bat and then belted his way to a great moment and a piece of baseball history.

The Shot Heard 'Round the World

The last-second home run is perhaps the single most dramatic great moment in baseball. When a player brings his team from the brink of defeat by blasting the ball into the distant stands, there is more emotion released on both sides than on any other single play.

Because baseball has such a long and glorious tradition, there has always been ample opportunity for the dramatic home run. And there have been many of them, home runs that have won games, pennants, and World Series. But of all the great moments created by the home run, one stands out head and shoulders above the rest. Without a doubt, this is the most well-known and most dramatic last-ditch home run ever hit. Even its nickname attests to its impact. It's known as the Shot Heard 'Round the World!

It happened back in 1951, and a great part of its drama came from the fact that it capped one of the most amazing comebacks ever seen in a pennant race. Add to that a pair of bitter rivals, the Brooklyn Dodgers and New York Giants, and the stage couldn't have been set in better fashion.

71

Baseball was a more intimate game back then. There were just sixteen teams, and none located west of St. Louis. Ironically, it would be the Dodgers and Giants who would initiate the change and expansion by moving to the West Coast in 1958. But in 1951, the two teams shared the New York spotlight with the American League Yankees. The Dodgers and Yanks were the dominant teams of the period, and when the Giants got in the middle, the fur was sure to fly.

The Yanks were on a roll. They had won it all in 1949 and 1950, and were well on their way to a third straight pennant in 1951. The Dodgers had been their World Series opponents in 1949, but in 1950, the "Whiz Kids" Philadelphia Phillies team edged them out. So in '51, the Dodgers were determined to regain the National League crown.

Most baseball fans know about the Dodger teams of the early fifties. They were star-studded aggregations featuring the likes of Pee Wee Reese, Duke Snider, Roy Campanella, Gil Hodges, Jackie Robinson, Carl Furillo, Billy Cox, Don Newcombe, and Preacher Roe among others. The Dodgers got off to a fast start in 1951, and it soon began to look as if they would run away and hide. For a time, it looked as if the Boston Braves might make a run at the Brooks, but they fell by the wayside. Then the Cardinals moved into second, but they, too, faltered.

Finally, it was the Giants who took up the chase, moving into second place. But it was a distant second, with most experts figuring that manager Leo Durocher's charges were too late to mount a serious challenge. The big problem was that the Giants had lost their first eleven games that year, giving them a tremendous early-season handicap to overcome.

But manager Durocher had been rebuilding his team since taking over in 1948, and he felt the '51 Giants could compete with anyone. His infield consisted of Whitey Lockman at first, Eddie Stanky at second, Alvin Dark at short, and Bobby Thomson at third. Wes Westrum was a solid catcher, and two of the starting outfielders were Monte Irvin and Don Mueller. The pitching staff was led by three veterans, Sal "The Barber" Maglie, Larry Jansen, and Jim Hearn.

When the Giants got off to that horrendous start, there were questions as to whether Durocher was on the right track. But Leo the Lip knew what he was doing, and early in the season he made a move that many feel completed the chemistry of the 1951 Giants. He called up a rookie centerfielder from the club's Minneapolis farm team, where the twenty-year-old was hitting a whopping .477. The youngster's name was Willie Mays, and he would become the most exciting player of his generation.

Mays didn't have a super rookie year. He was to hit just .274 in 121 games, but his 20 homers and 68 RBIs helped the cause, and his outstanding play in the outfield solidified the club defensively. Soon after Mays joined the team, the Giants began moving toward second place. But the Dodgers were still far ahead.

By the All-Star Game that year, the majority of baseball people proclaimed the National League race over, and were already anticipating yet another Dodger-Yankee World Series. And by mid-August, with some 44 games remaining, the Dodgers had a big 13½-game lead over the Giants. Even Brooklyn manager Charley Dressen said he felt the Giants were out of it.

But that's when an amazing thing began to happen. The Giants started winning and winning big, while the Dodgers began to look like just another .500 team, winning one, then losing one. Thus the gap was closing, and by September it looked as if there might be a pennant race after all, especially when a Giant 16-game winning streak sliced the Brooklyn lead to five games.

By the time the final game of the season rolled around, the two clubs were in a dead heat. The Giants played the Boston Braves that day, and Larry Jansen beat them, 3–2. Now the outcome of the pennant race hinged on the result of the Dodgers-Phillies game, still in progress. The Giants players sat down to wait. They had done their job, winning 37 of those final 44 games, and putting themselves in the driver's seat for the first time all year.

The Brooklyn-Philadelphia game was a wild affair. Tied at 8–8 after nine, it went into extra innings, and in the 12th the Phillies loaded the bases when their first baseman, Eddie Waitkus, hit a low liner that seemed ticketed for the hole between first and second. If it went through, the Phillies would win the game and the Giants would take the pennant.

But the Dodgers' great second baseman, Jackie Robinson, took several quick steps to his left, dove through the air, and made an incredible catch of the low liner to retire the side. Two innings later, in the 14th, Robinson hit a clutch home run that ultimately gave the Dodgers a 9–8 victory and enabled them to tie the Giants once more. Now the two teams would meet in a best-of-three playoff to decide the National League championship.

The first game was held at Ebbets Field in Brooklyn, and it looked as if the pattern of the second half of the season would continue. The Giants won, 3–1, behind Jim Hearn, as third baseman Bobby Thomson had three hits, including his 31st home run of the season. The Dodgers suffered another blow when their catcher, Roy Campanella, injured a leg and was declared out for the remainder of the playoffs. The Giants certainly seemed to be in the driver's seat.

But the next day, at the Polo Grounds, the Giants' home field, Brooklyn got even. Rookie Clem Labine pitched a six-hit shutout and the Dodgers won easily, 10–0. Now it was down to one game for the pennant. It would also be played at the Polo Grounds and would match a pair of 20-game winners, Don Newcombe of the Dodgers and the Giants' Sal Maglie.

A Robinson single gave the Dodgers a 1–0 lead in the first and it stayed that way until the seventh, when the Giants tied it on a fly out by Thomson, allowing Monte Irvin to score. With two innings left, the tension was building. It was still anyone's game and, consequently, anyone's pennant.

But in the top of the eighth, it looked as if disaster has struck the Giants. Reese and Snider singled off Maglie to start the inning. A wild pitch brought Reese home with the tie-breaking run. Then Robinson walked. The next batter, Andy Pafko, singled off Thomson's glove at third, bringing Snider home and making it a 3–1 game. After Gil Hodges was retired, Billy Cox bounced one to third. It took a weird hop off Thomson's shoulder and bounced into leftfield. Robinson raced home with the third run of the inning, making it a 4–1 game.

Now things really looked bleak for the Giants. Had they come so far only to lose in the final game of the season? The fans at the Polo Grounds booed Bobby Thomson for his spotty fielding. Maglie finally got out of the inning, but the three runs had given the Dodgers a comfortable cushion. And the Giants only had six outs left.

When Newcombe set the Giants down with no trouble in the eighth, it looked even worse. Only a miracle could save the Giants now, and miracles don't happen very often. Larry Jansen pitched the top of the ninth for the Giants, and it was still a 4–1 game as the Jints prepared for what could be their final at bat of the 1951 season.

Shortstop Alvin Dark led off with a single. And when Don Mueller followed with a base hit, the Giants fans began coming alive. Now Monte Irvin was up. He had been the Giants' top run producer with more than 120 RBIs, but this time Newcombe got him to pop to Hodges at first. Now Dodger fans breathed a sigh of relief. The emotional ebb and flow was incredible.

First baseman Whitey Lockman was up. He caught a Newcombe fastball and whacked it to left for a double, scoring Dark and sending Mueller to third, where he injured an ankle sliding and had to be removed on a stretcher. Clint Hartung was the pinch runner, but more importantly, it was now a 4–2 game. The tying runs were in scoring position. The Giants were definitely alive. Manager Charley Dressen decided to make a pitching change. He called for big righthander Ralph Branca to replace Newcombe.

The Shot Heard 'Round the World—Bobby Thomson connects with a Ralph Branca pitch and belts the home run that wins the pennant for the 1951 New York Giants over the Brooklyn Dodgers.

Branca had joined the Dodgers as an eighteen-year-old back in 1944, getting an early start because so many veterans were in the service. Three years later, as a twenty-one-year-old, Branca won 21 games, but in the years just prior to '51 he did not do as well, having a 7–9 mark in 1950 and a 12–12 log so far in '51. But as he walked in from the bullpen on that cool October afternoon, Ralph Branca was thinking about how he'd pitch to the next batter, Bobby Thomson.

Thomson, too, must have been thinking. Here he was, coming up in the biggest clutch situation of his life. Everything the club had worked for was on the line. He also knew that his fielding lapses had helped prolong the Dodger rally. So he came to the plate with one thought in mind—to get a base hit and keep things going. The on-deck hitter was rookie Willie Mays. To this day, people wonder what would have happened if Mays had come to bat.

But that wasn't to be. After taking Branca's first pitch, Thomson got set again. The big righthander tried to come inside with a fastball, but it was in the strike zone and Thomson swung. CRACK! It was the unmistakable sound of solid contact, as Thomson hit a wicked line drive toward the leftfield grandstand. Everyone in New York and Brooklyn held their breath. Would the ball be high enough to clear the leftfield wall?

It did. It was a three-run homer. The Giants had come back from the dead to win the game . . . and the pennant! Bobby Thomson had hit one of the most dramatic home runs in baseball history. The Polo Grounds went absolutely berserk as Ralph Branca walked sadly from the mound. He would forever be linked with Thomson now as part of baseball history. He was the man who gave up THE home run.

As Thomson circled the bases, or in his words, "rode around them on a cloud," Giants announcer Russ Hodges screamed over the microphone to all of New York.

"THE GIANTS WIN THE PENNANT! THE GIANTS WIN THE PENNANT! THE GIANTS WIN THE PENNANT!"

That said it all. The homer had capped an already incredible comeback story. It was the perfect icing on the cake. The Shot Heard 'Round the World. As great a moment as there had ever been in baseball.

The Big Train Finally Gets His Wish

Do people ever feel sorry for a superstar? Not very often. But there are a number of situations that do evoke sympathy, even for the great player. One of them would be the result of an injury, when a superstar cannot perform in his usual way or must retire prematurely because he is hurt. Another occurs when a very great player must toil year after year for a poor or mediocre team, and never find his way into a World Series or championship game.

This has happened with a number of great players in all the major sports. Then there are those who finally get to the big break late in their career, and the question arises whether they will at long last come out on top. One of the earliest examples of this in baseball involves one of the greatest pitchers in the whole history of the game. He waited for eighteen long years to get into a World Series. But once he got there, he found that winning that elusive Series game would not be an easy task.

The pitcher in question is none other than Walter Johnson, the immortal Big Train, whose 416 lifetime victories are second only to Cy Young on the all-time list. To mention all Johnson's accomplishments would take too much time. Suffice to say that the Big Train was the more feared fastball pitcher of his time. Some still call him the fastest ever. He holds the record for lifetime shutouts with 113, and until recent years when both Nolan Ryan and Steve Carlton passed him, was the all-time strikeout leader with 3,508.

Though there wasn't a mean bone in Johnson's body, opposing players nevertheless feared his fastball. They knew Walter wouldn't throw at them, but if one slipped and came in high and hard . . . No one wanted to think about the consequences. Even the great Ty Cobb, the most fearless player in the game, once gave this answer when asked about his most embarrassing moment in baseball.

Said the Georgia Peach: "Facing Walter Johnson on any dark day in Washington."

That in itself says a great deal. It serves to define Walter Johnson's great power and also perhaps his greatest problem, though a loyal man like Walter never really complained. But the Big Train's entire career was spent in Washington, with the old Senators. Twenty-one seasons with a team that rarely finished in the first division. Based in the nation's capital, the old joke about the club went like this: "Washington. First in war, first in peace, and *last* in the American League."

That wasn't far from the truth. Yet pitching for all those bad Senator teams, Walter Johnson won 20 or more games on twelve separate occasions. In two of those seasons he won more than 30, putting together an incredible 36–7 record in 1913, throwing 12 shutouts and finishing with an earned run average of just 1.14.

Yet he often did it with little batting support from his teammates. That was why, people often said, he pitched so many shutouts. It was the only way he could be sure of winning. In fact, Walter Johnson was involved in sixty-four 1–0 decisions in his career. He won thirty-eight of them, but the rest were heartbreaking defeats. That's what pitching for the lowly Senators could do.

And, of course, Walter never got the chance to pitch in a World Series. For a while, it looked as if he never would. One year, 1916, the Senators were so bad that Walter lost 20 games. He won 25, but had all those losses despite a glittering earned run average of 1.89.

By 1920, Walter Johnson's powerful right arm had thrown a lot of pitches. He was thirty-three years old, and he came up with the first sore arm of his career. He finished with just an 8–10 record, and in the three seasons after that wasn't the pitcher he had been before, with records of 17–14, 15–16, and 17–12. Coming into the 1924 season, the Big Train was past his thirty-sixth birthday and many thought the end was near. The irony was that the Senators finally had a contending team.

But with the prospect of a possible pennant, Walter Johnson turned back the clock. He finished with an outstanding, 23–7 record and helped pitch the Senators to the American League pennant. He would be in the World Series at last. The Senators would be meeting the powerful New York Giants, who were heavy favorites.

It surprised no one when Walter Johnson was the Senator pitcher in the opening game. He pitched valiantly, but as usual, got very little hitting support from his teammates. The game was tied at 2–2 at the end of nine, and the Giants finally pushed across a couple against Johnson in the 12th. Washington got one back, but lost the game, 4–3. Walter pitched courageously, striking out twelve, but how much more life could there be in his aging arm?

He took the mound again in game five with the Series knotted at two games each. Only this time he didn't have his good stuff and lost, 6–2. It was beginning to look as if after waiting eighteen years, the old man wasn't going to win a World Series game after all. Then the Senators fought back and won game six, forcing a seventh and deciding contest in Washington.

Johnson, of course, had pitched just two days earlier and couldn't start. But when the Senators overcame a 3–1 deficit to tie the game in the eighth inning, manager Bucky Harris brought Walter Johnson into the fray. He was not only placing his team's destiny in the hands of the Big Train, but he was giving Walter a final chance to win a game in the Series.

With the world championship on the line, Walter Johnson again showed why many have called him the best ever. For four innings he called on every bit of power his aging arm could muster to hold the Giants. And each time he walked off the mound, he hoped his team could get the run that would mean victory.

Finally, in the bottom of the 12th, the Senators got something going. Muddy Ruel, given a second life when Giant catcher Hank Gowdy tripped on his own mask while trying to catch Ruel's pop foul, blasted a double. Earl McNeeley then hit a hard grounder to third, which took a bad hop over Fred Lindstrom's head, allowing Ruel to race home with the winning run.

The Senators were champions, and Lady Luck had

83

at long last smiled upon Walter Johnson. He had finally won a World Series game, achieving his final goal as a player. All his teammates congratulated him, as a smiling Big Train basked in the glory of his great moment.

There is a postscript to the story, however. The next year, 1925, Walter again won 20 games and led his club to a second pennant. Pitching in the Series once more, he was brilliant. He whipped the Pittsburgh Pirates in game one, 4–1, then shut them out in game four, 4–0. So he had won three Series games now, but the last one got away.

Pitching in the seventh and deciding game, the Big Train was betrayed by the weather. The field was soaked by an all-day rain and it came down during most of the game. Johnson had trouble both on the slippery mound and in gripping the ball. He went the entire nine innings, only to lose, 9–7. Afterward, manager Bucky Harris was criticized for staying with the aging veteran for so long. But Harris defended his decision, and in doing so perhaps best summed up the essence of Walter Johnson.

"There's no man in the world I'd rather have on the mound than Walter Johnson," he said. "When you're in a big game, you go with your best. And Walter's the best there is."

A Happy/Sad Ending

Sing no sad songs for Sandy Koufax. He wouldn't want it that way. After all, he was a very great pitcher, a record setter, a Hall of Famer, a man who dominated the game in the final five years of his career. During that time, he was as good as any pitcher who ever lived. The rub is that Sandy Koufax was forced to retire just prior to his thirty-first birthday. As it turned out, his final season in baseball, 1966, was his very greatest.

Sandy Koufax was a pitcher who specialized in great moments. He was the author of a then record-breaking four no-hitters, one of them a perfect game. While he was still trying to find his pitching legs back in 1959, he went out one day and fanned eighteen batters, tying the record at that time. He pitched in eight World Series games and had an earned run average of 0.95. He was a National League Most Valuable Player and he won the Cy Young Award as the league's best pitcher on three occasions.

Yet despite all the impressive credentials, Sandy Koufax spent the first six years of his career as a losing pitcher, a flame-throwing lefty who couldn't get it together. His record for those years was just 36–40, and for a time it looked as if he'd be nothing more than a .500 pitcher.

But when Sandy Koufax finally put it together, he had no equal. His final six years produced a 129–47 mark, and that would have been even better had it not been for two major ailments, the second leading to his premature retirement following the 1966 season.

In his prime, Sandy Koufax had a blazing fastball, which he mixed with a sharp-breaking curve and surprisingly effective change-up. On top of that, he had a fluid motion and the kind of stamina that allowed him to be as strong in the ninth inning as he was in the first. At 6'2" and 200 pounds, he had the good size, and was even stronger than he looked.

His back was a mass of muscle, muscle that tended to tighten when he'd tense up on the mound, as he did so often in his early years. During his entire career the Dodger trainers had to work on him to keep the muscles loose, and Sandy himself often did bending and stretching exercises on the mound between pitches and between hitters.

He joined the Dodgers as a nineteen-year-old when the club was still based in Brooklyn in 1955. Because of the different rules back then, the Dodgers couldn't farm him out for fear of losing him. So he was part of the Brooklyn World Series winning team in 1955 and pennant-winning club in '56. But he contributed little. He started seeing more action when the club moved to Los Angeles in 1958, but he was still wild and often erratic. He thought he was getting it together in 1959 when he fanned eighteen in a game and had an 8–6 mark. But the next year he fell back to 8–13 and was really discouraged.

That's when Norm Sherry stepped in. Sherry was the Dodgers' third-string catcher, and in the spring of 1961 he was getting ready to catch Sandy in a "B" squad game. Before the action started, Sherry had a little talk with his pitcher. He told Sandy to relax, not to try to blow the ball past every hitter. He also suggested Sandy throw with an easier motion and that he use his curve and change more often.

"Don't be afraid to be a pitcher," Sherry said.

The formula worked. For the first time, Sandy felt comfortable on the mound. Whenever he began to tense up, Sherry would go out and talk to him. And they found that without the tenseness, Sandy was throwing nearly as hard and the ball had more natural movement, more hop.

Sandy became a star almost overnight. He went from an 8–13 mark in 1960 to an 18–13 record in '61. And the next year he proved it was for real. By June 30, he had a 10–4 mark, and that night he pitched a no-hitter against the New York Mets. He seemed to be getting better and better. But even then, there was trouble.

Sandy had broken an artery in the fleshy part of his left hand, causing the circulation to his index finger to be partially blocked. The finger was often numb. He won three more games to bring his record to 14–4. That's when the circulation to his finger stopped. For a time, it was thought the finger might have to be amputated. That would have ended things right then and there. But the finger gradually improved. He made a few late-season starts, but was ineffective, and his final record was 14–7.

Then came 1963 and Sandy's first super season. He

was 25–5 with 306 strikeouts and a 1.88 earned run average, unquestionably the best pitcher in baseball. He won a pair of World Series games that year as the Dodgers swept the New York Yankees, won the Cy Young Award and the MVP. His turnaround was complete. At the age of twenty-eight, he appeared to have nearly a decade of great pitching ahead of him.

He was just as good the next year, once again looking practically unbeatable. Then in a game against Milwaukee on August 8, he dove back into second base on a pickoff attempt and landed hard on his left elbow. The soreness was worse than usual the next day, but Sandy figured it was just part of pitching, along with a bruise.

On August 20, he threw a 3–0 whitewash against the Cardinals, striking out thirteen, and showing no effects of the elbow bruise of two weeks earlier. His record was up to 19–5. The man was simply amazing. Sandy went to bed that night totally unaware of what would await him in the morning. He related the memory of that morning in his own words.

"I had to drag my arm out of bed like a log," he said. "That's what it looked like, a log. A waterlogged log. Where it had been swollen outside the joint before, it was now swollen all the way from the shoulder down to the wrist—inside, outside, everywhere. For an elbow, I had a knee. That's how thick it was."

After a series of medical tests, Sandy Koufax got the bad news. For one thing, his season was over. He'd stop at 19–5 with 223 strikeouts in 223 innings and a sensational 1.74 ERA. That's the kind of year he was building on. But that wasn't the worst part.

He was suffering from traumatic arthritis in the

Dodger great Sandy Koufax, the dominant pitcher of the 1960s. In his final year, he pitched for a 27–9 season with 317 strikeouts and a 1.73 E.R.A., while earning his third Cy Young award.

elbow. It was something brought about by the wear and tear of pitching. The cartilage was being chipped away gradually. The dive into the base in Milwaukee just hastened the onset of the symptoms. And it was an irreversible condition. As long as Sandy pitched, it would continue to get worse.

This is why the final two seasons of Sandy Koufax's career were so incredible. While he was producing one great moment after another, very few people knew what Sandy was putting himself through. Besides the pain, there was the knowledge that each game he pitched might be his last. Of course, opposing hitters would have said that it was nonsense. There couldn't be anything wrong with Sandy's arm. He was mowing them down as never before.

But what he began doing in 1965 was to skip throwing between starts. That way, the arm and elbow had more time to recover from the strain of pitching. He also had to take painkillers after a game, had many sleepless nights, and often had to have the elbow drained. Ironically, he was most free of pain when he actually pitched. Throwing his still-incredible fastball seemed to provide some relief. It was between starts that he suffered the most agonizing pain.

Yet in 1965 he threw the most innings of his career, 336. His record was 26–8, and he set a mark of 382 strikeouts for the season. His earned run average was 2.04, and he tossed his fourth no-hitter, a perfect game against the Chicago Cubs. Ernie Banks, the longtime star with the Cubs, was simply amazed that day. "Koufax just tried to throw the ball past us," Banks said, "and he did."

The Dodgers found themselves in another World

Series that year, and Sandy was the star. In game two, he gave up two runs in six innings, only one of them earned, but lost, 5–1, the relief pitching allowing the final three Minnesota tallies. Then in game five he shut out the Twins on four hits, 7–0, and coming back with just two days rest, he shut them out again, winning the seventh and deciding game, 2–0, while giving up just three hits. It was still another great moment. His earned run average for the three World Series games was a minuscule 0.38!

He also took his second Cy Young Award after the season. Yet in spite of being nearly two months short of his thirtieth birthday, Sandy was already thinking about retirement. What it came down to was just how much pain he was able to endure, how much more strain he was willing to put on his left arm. He finally decided to try it again in 1966.

The results were the same. There was the pain, the pills, the needles . . . and the brilliant pitching. Fans around the National League still flocked to the park when the Dodgers were in town and Koufax was scheduled to pitch. None of them was aware of the courageous performance being put on by Sandy Koufax every time he took the mound. All they knew was that he mowed the hitters down like no other pitcher in the game. He was the absolute best. No doubt about it.

Once again he produced a brilliant, record-breaking season, filled with great moments. He threw another 323 innings, compiled a 27–9 record with 317 strikeouts. His earned run average was a career best 1.73. He didn't miss a turn, and once more pitched his team into the World Series.

Sandy and the Dodgers ran out of luck in the Fall

Classic that year, mainly because the bats went silent. The Dodgers scored two runs in the first game, then were shut out three straight times by the young Baltimore Oriole pitchers, to complete a Series sweep. What would turn out to be Sandy's final big league appearance was a loss. Typically, he gave up just one earned run in six innings, but with no runs, not even Sandy Koufax could produce a victory.

Yet shortly after the season ended, he won his third Cy Young prize, and solidified his reputation as the best of his generation. Then about two months after the season ended, Sandy Koufax called a press conference. What he was about to tell an unsuspecting press and public would shock the sports world.

Sandy Koufax was about to announce his retirement from baseball. In view of his unprecedented pitching success over the past five seasons, and the fact that he could have continued and perhaps even had a few more super seasons, his courageous decision may have been his greatest moment of them all.

"Let's say I've had a few too many shots and pills because of this arm," he said. "I don't want to take a chance of disabling myself. I don't have a moment's regret for my twelve years in the big leagues, but I could regret one season too many.

"So what I'm saying is that I want to live the rest of my life with complete use of my body."

Then, for the first time, Sandy told everyone just what he had gone through while he was winning game after game. He explained that his arm was deteriorating, that it was already beginning to shorten, and when he went to shave his face he couldn't reach with his arm unless he bent over.

It was a chilling story, one that probed beneath the surface glamour so often associated with professional sports. When it ended, Sandy Koufax walked away, just as he had walked off the mound so often in the past five years—a winner.

The Greatest Miracle Moment
of Them All

One of the big popular music hits of the early 1950s was a song called "Rags to Riches." The song did not tell the story of a baseball team. But if someone did want to make a baseball club the subject of a song using that title, there would be just one team that would qualify overwhelmingly as the subject. It would have to be the 1969 version of the New York Mets, a team that wrote the ultimate script of a rags-to-riches story in sports. And in doing so, they produced a great moment never to be forgotten.

Look at it as an old-fashioned fairy tale. Once upon a time there were three major league baseball teams in New York City—the Yankees, Dodgers, and Giants. But after the 1957 season, two of them went away. That was when the Giants and Dodgers decided to move west and seek their fortunes in California. That left only the Yankees, and in a city the size of New York there was room for more. So in 1962 a new franchise was born. Welcome to the National League, New York Mets.

The rest of the National League was very happy to see the Mets join their family. Why? Well, the Mets were the perfect team to play when you wanted to win some games, fatten your batting average, lower your earned run average, and build your confidence. You see, the infant New York Mets were terrible, a baseball team hard pressed to win. On the contrary, the Mets specialized in losing. They found more ways to lose than any team before them.

In their initial season, the New York Mets set a record by losing 120 ballgames. The only highlight all year long was their manager, the venerable and beloved Casey Stengel. Ol' Case or the Ol' Perfesser, as he was called, had been the highly successful field leader of the New York Yankees throughout most of the 1950s. He had proven he could win when he had the talent, so no one blamed him for losing. They just enjoyed his baseball wisdom and the special way he had of conversing. Stengelese, the writers called it.

"Come and see my amazing Mets," Ol' Case would proclaim, "which in some cases have played only semi-pro ball."

Stengel had unwittingly given the club a nickname that has stuck to this day. Win or lose, good or bad, they will always be the Amazin' Mets. But in the early days they mostly lost. The first four seasons the Mets were perennial cellar-dwellers. Stengel retired after the 1965 season and former Giants catcher Wes Westrum took command.

Playing under Westrum, the Mets made a move in 1966. They actually escaped the basement and finished ninth in a ten-team league. But a year later, 1967, they were back in last place. Only there was a difference. The club had discovered a pitcher . . . and a leader. A strong-armed, twenty-two-year-old rookie named Tom Seaver had won 16 games.

Then in '68 the club had another new manager. He was Gil Hodges, already a hero in New York from his playing days with the Brooklyn Dodgers. Hodges led the club to another ninth-place finish in '68. But the Mets weren't far from the basement and to many people still the laughingstock of the league.

But there were subtle differences. Seaver had won 16 games once again, and he was joined by a twenty-five-year-old lefthander named Jerry Koosman who won 19. With more young arms waiting in the wings, there was the making of a real pitching staff. In addition, there were a number of other young players capable of doing the job, such as catcher Jerry Grote, outfielders Cleon Jones and Tommy Agee, and shortstop Bud Harrelson. So as 1969 approached there were those who felt the Mets might make a move, and maybe get another notch or two higher in the standings.

There was another big change as the 1969 season approached. The National League had expanded from ten to twelve teams, and for the first time was split into two divisions of six teams each. So now there would be two divisional winners who would have to meet in a playoff series to determine the pennant winner. But the Mets wouldn't have to worry about that. Oh, yeah? Rags-to-riches time was about to begin.

The Mets didn't get off to a lightning start that year, but they were holding their own. Seaver was proving to be perhaps the best pitcher in baseball, and after some early-season arm problems, Koosman was winning, too. Another rookie, Gary Gentry, was giving the staff a big lift, while veteran Don Cardwell was proving an able fourth starter. The pitching became the heart of the team.

But that wasn't all. The club was strong up the middle defensively, with catcher Grote, shortstop Harrelson, and centerfielder Agee. A midseason trade brought power hitter Donn Clendenon to the club, while young veterans Ron Swoboda and Ed Kranepool also provided punch. Leftfielder Jones was up among the batting leaders all year long. The club was getting a good feeling about itself, and moving up in the standings.

Long-suffering Mets fans began to ride the bandwagon as the club surged into second place in August and began to chase the front-running Chicago Cubs. Could this really be happening? Suddenly, the Mets could do no wrong. Every move manager Hodges made seemed to be the right one, and the two young pitching aces, Seaver and Koosman, were getting harder and harder to beat.

In early September, the New Yorkers whipped the fading Cubs two straight. It was part of a 10-game winning streak that culminated with a doubleheader victory over Montreal on September 10. That was the day the Mets went into first place for the very first time in the franchise history. They were writing a Cinderella story and the entire sports world was watching. Could it really be happening, or would the New Yorkers crash back to earth with a loud thud?

But they continued to win. Then on the night of September 24, rookie Gentry shut out the Cardinals, 6–0, to clinch the divisional title, and the city of New York went wild. The Mets had completed the first part of their odyssey, which was already leading many people to feel the Amazins were truly a team of destiny.

The Mets finished September with an incredible 23–

7 mark, and from mid-August to the end of the season they were 37–10. The perennial cellar-dwellers had compiled a 100–62 record for the season. Seaver had a Cy Young Award year with a 25–7 record. Koosman was 17–9, and rookie Gentry 13–12. Cleon Jones batted .340, while Agee smacked 26 home runs. Clendenon also provided timely power after coming to the club at midseason. But more important than the stats, the team always seemed to come through in the clutch.

Whenever there was a big hit needed, someone got it. Whenever a victory demanded a clutch pitching performance, it was there. Whenever manager Hodges made a defensive change, or put in a pinch hitter, it seemed to be the right move. It was almost uncanny, almost . . . out of this world.

Typical of the Mets season was a game against St. Louis on September 15. That night, a young St. Louis lefty named Steve Carlton was simply sensational. He established a new major league record by striking out nineteen Mets. There was only one problem. He lost! Yep. Even that night the Mets had the magic. Ron Swoboda hit a pair of two-run homers between all the strikeouts and the New Yorkers won, 4–3. Team of destiny? Who was to argue.

So the New York Mets had gone from ninth place in 1968 all the way to first in '69. A team that had finished in the basement five of its previous seven years was now close to being on top of the baseball world. Had it been a year earlier, the Mets would have gone right on to the World Series. But 1969, with divisional play, demanded a best-of-three playoff series. The winner of that won the pennant and advanced to the Series.

The Western Division winner that year was the Atlanta Braves. Though the Braves hadn't won as many regular season games as the Mets, they were a hard-hitting veteran team favored to end the Mets' dream. Atlanta had such noted sluggers as Henry Aaron, Orlando Cepeda, and Rico Carty. The club also had a 23-game winner in Phil Niekro. The city of Atlanta was sky-high. After all, their team would easily dispose of the Mets and be headed for the World Series.

Of course, it didn't happen that way. It was the Mets who turned into sluggers and disposed of the mighty Braves in three straight by scores of 9–5, 11–6, and 7–4. Even weak-hitting infielders were belting the ball out of sight. Team of destiny? It was certainly beginning to look that way.

When the Mets clinched their first-ever pennant at Shea Stadium, the fans went wild. They started yet another tradition—ripping up the field. Huge chunks of Shea Stadium sod were pulled up as the pennant-happy fans wanted souvenirs of their team's finest hour. But there was still one step remaining. A major one—the World Series. And waiting for the Mets was the ac-knowledged best team in baseball—the Baltimore Orioles.

The O's had run away with the American League, winning their division by 19 games and taking 109 victories during the regular season. They had a star-studded lineup from top to bottom and a great pitching staff. There was Frank and Brooks Robinson, Boog Powell, Paul Blair, Don Buford, Mark Belanger, Davey Johnson, Dave McNally, Jim Palmer, Mike Cuellar, and last, but not least, their dynamic little manager Earl Weaver. It was a great team, heavily favored to take the Series and end the Mets' dream.

The Fall Classic opened at Baltimore's Memorial Stadium on October 11. The Birds went with 23-game winner Mike Cuellar, while the Mets countered with their ace, Tom Seaver. After the Mets went quietly in the first, leftfielder Don Buford stepped up to lead off for the O's. Buford took a pitch, then deposited Seaver's next delivery into the rightfield seats for a home run. As the Oriole fans went wild, Mets rooters had to be wondering. Was this the beginning of the end?

It was still 1–0 in the Oriole fourth. That's when the bottom of the order got to Seaver. Shortstop Belanger drove home a run. Then Cuellar helped his own cause with an RBI. Finally Buford whacked a double to get another home. Now the Orioles had a 4–0 lead. Seaver left after the fifth inning and Cuellar coasted to an easy, 4–1 victory. The Orioles had jumped on top.

Many writers and fans thought the Oriole triumph would serve to dishearten the Mets. After all, their best pitcher had been beaten and perhaps now the players themselves would stop believing the "team of destiny" line. Now, many felt, the young Mets would crumble like a paper tiger.

Game two matched another Baltimore 20-game winner, Dave McNally, against the Mets' Jerry Koosman. It was a scoreless pitchers' battle until the fourth inning, when New York's Donn Clendenon blasted a home run to make it 1–0. After six innings it was still a 1–0 game. Koosman had been brilliant and the Orioles still didn't have a single hit. But in the seventh, centerfielder Paul Blair broke the spell with a single. He then stole second and came home on a single by Brooks Robinson and the game was tied at 1–1.

It was still knotted in the ninth. An Oriole victory

here and the Mets might really crack. But with two down in the top of the inning, Mets third baseman Ed Charles rapped a single. Catcher Grote followed with another base hit, and then the normally weak-hitting Al Weis clipped a single to right, driving home Charles with the go-ahead run.

The Orioles threatened briefly in the bottom of the inning, but veteran Ron Taylor came on to retire Brooks Robinson to end the ballgame. The Mets had evened things up and the two teams moved to Shea Stadium for game three, with rookie Gary Gentry opposing the Orioles' Jim Palmer. This time the Mets wasted no time. Agee homered in the first, and pitcher Gentry drove home a pair in the second, making it a 3–0 game. Then, in the fourth, something happened that began to make people think all over again that the Mets, indeed, were a team of destiny.

With two outs, the Orioles put a pair of baserunners on, and catcher Elrod Hendricks drove one deep into the left-centerfield gap. Centerfielder Agee, who was shading to right for the lefthand hitter, raced after the ball at full speed. As he neared the wall at the 396-foot marker, Agee lunged, stretching his gloved hand across his body. The ball had actually fallen past his head, then his chest. But as it was passing his waist, he caught it in the webbing of his glove and held on as he hit the wall.

Agee turned and held his glove in the air for all to see. There was the ball, still balancing unsteadily in the tip of the webbing. It had been a miraculous catch and now it was the Orioles turn to wonder just what they had to do to beat this club. But just to show it wasn't a fluke, Agee did it again in the seventh.

It was a 4–0 game by then, but the Orioles loaded the bases with two out and Paul Blair up. Manager Hodges yanked Gentry in favor of fastballer Nolan Ryan, who was sometimes spectacular, but often wild. Blair jumped on a Ryan fastball and drove it into right-center. Again, Agee had a long run as the Orioles runners circled the bases. At the last second he dove headfirst and caught the ball just before it hit the ground.

The Shea Stadium crowd went berserk and the Mets went on to a 5–0 victory and 2–1 lead in the Series. Credit this one to Agee. Had he failed to make either catch, the Mets would have been in trouble. Now it was Tom Seaver and Mike Cuellar again in game four. The Oriole players were still confident, at least outwardly.

"They're not supermen," Brooks Robinson said. "They're just flesh and blood. Our turn will come, you'll see."

But it was the Mets who drew first blood. In the second inning Donn Clendenon slammed his second homer of the Series to give the Mets a 1–0 lead. Then both pitchers started throwing goose eggs. Coming into the ninth inning it was still a 1–0 game. Seaver was just three outs away from a shutout victory.

With one out, however, the Orioles came to life. Frank Robinson and Boog Powell singled, putting runners on first and third. Now Brooks Robinson was up, and he drove one into the right-centerfield gap. If it fell safely, the Orioles would probably take the lead. Agee was chasing the ball again, but he was too far this time. Then, out of nowhere, came rightfielder Ron Swoboda. The big guy, never noted for his fielding, dove headfirst, stretched his left arm out in front of him, and speared

The 1969 New York Mets celebrate moments after clinching their World Series upset over the Baltimore Orioles.

the ball at ground level. It was impossible catch number three. Although Robinson tagged and came home with the tying run, the catch prevented further damage and Seaver got out of the inning.

The Mets couldn't score in their half of the inning and it went to extras. But the way the New Yorkers were producing great moments, it seemed as if there was no way they could lose. They proved it in the bottom of the tenth. A fly lost in the sun that went for a double, a walk, and a misplayed bunt led to the run that won the ballgame for Seaver and the Mets. It was now 3–1 in games and beginning to look like a fairytale ending after all.

Game five had Jerry Koosman returning to the mound against Dave McNally. It was scoreless until the third when McNally surprised everyone and helped his own cause with a two-run homer. Then, with two out, Frank Robinson hit a tremendous shot into the seats to increase the lead to 3–0. Maybe the Orioles were finally coming back?

Though just a second-year player, Jerry Koosman didn't rattle. He settled down and began retiring the Orioles with no further damage. In the sixth, the Mets' magic returned. Cleon Jones claimed he was hit by a pitch and manager Hodges proved it by showing the umpire a shoe-polish smudge on the ball. With Jones on first, Donn Clendenon blasted his third homer of the Series to make it a 3–2 game. The more than 57,000 fans jammed into Shea began to get excited. Perhaps they were about to see the Mets win the Series after all.

In the seventh it was magic time again. Light-hitting Al Weis turned tiger and blasted a home run over the leftfield fence. His unlikely shot drew the Mets even at 3–3. Then came the eighth inning. Back-to-back doubles by Jones and Swoboda broke the tie, and a misplay by first baseman Powell allowed a second run to score. It was now 5–3, and suddenly the Orioles had just three outs left.

Koosman toed the rubber, knowing the Mets' destiny was riding on his strong left arm. He faltered momentarily, walking Frank Robinson to start the inning. But then Powell hit into a fielder's choice and Brooks Robinson skyed to right. One out left and second baseman Davey Johnson up. Johnson hit a lazy fly to left. Cleon Jones camped under it, and as he squeezed the ball in his glove, he went down on one knee, as if to say thanks. Thanks for making the New York Mets champions of the baseball world!

They were a team that turned baseball upside down with an improbable season and championship run that still makes the experts blink. Never have the odds against a team been so high, from the first day of the year to the final out of the World Series. The Mets became a team of twenty-five great moments. The lightning could strike from anywhere.

In a final irony, Davey Johnson, the Oriole second baseman who made the final out on that fateful October day in 1969, became a big league manager in the early 1980s. The team he is managing is none other than the New York Mets. Team of destiny? Maybe the whole thing was planned out back in 1969.

One Strike Away—
The Incredible 1986
Playoffs and World Series

One of the most tantalizing aspects of the game of baseball is that you never know just when a great moment will occur. It can happen during a routine midseason game that might have no bearing on the pennant races. Or it can happen in the thick of a pennant fight, or better yet, in the Playoffs or World Series.

And when this happens, both avid baseball fans and casual observers alike are equally caught up in the excitement. National television has seen to that. Perhaps this has never been more clearly demonstrated than in the recent 1986 Playoffs and World Series. Baseball was on its post-season center stage, and the electricity produced by the New York Mets, Boston Red Sox, Houston Astros, and California Angels kept fans all over the country on the edge of their seats.

The Mets-Astros series was expected to be hotly contested, since the two clubs had been bitter rivals since entering the National League as expansion teams in 1962. The Mets, who won 108 games during the regular season, were widely acknowledged as the best team in baseball during 1986. But experts agreed that the Astros had the front-line pitching to stop them.

In the American League, the gritty Boston Red Sox would be taking on the aging California Angels. The Bosox, who had beaten back every challenge to hold first place in the American League East during the regular season, were favored to beat the California team with its veteran cast of post–thirty-year-olds. But the Red Sox were also playing against their own history. The club hadn't won a World Series in some 68 years, with recent failings in 1946, 1967, and 1975. Could they break the jinx in '86?

So there were a number of questions to be answered on all sides when the two playoff series began. The Mets-Astros series began in Houston with a tight pitchers' battle. When the smoke cleared, Astros' ace Mike Scott came away with a 1–0 victory over the Mets' already legendary twenty-one-year-old, Dwight Gooden. The game's only run came on a Glenn Davis homer. Scott was completely dominant, striking out 14 and feasting on the heart of the New York lineup—Keith Hernandez, Gary Carter, Darryl Strawberry, and Ray Knight.

The Mets evened things in the second game, when Bob Ojeda beat veteran Nolan Ryan, 5–1. It wasn't until the series returned to New York that the excitement really began to heat up. Ron Darling started for the Mets against Bob Knepper of Houston. By the end of the second Houston was leading 4–0, and the Mets

1986 National League Cy Young Award winner Mike Scott of the Houston Astros. Scott dominated the New York Mets in two playoff games. The Mets won the series in six games, and avoided facing Scott for a third time.

looked in trouble. But the New Yorkers tied it in the sixth, highlighted by Darryl Strawberry's three-run homer. The Astros scratched for a run in the seventh, and going into the ninth held a slim 5–4 lead.

Relief ace Dave Smith was on the mound for the Astros as the Mets' Wally Backman led off with a bunt single, making a nifty slide to avoid the tag. He went to second on a passed ball before pinch hitter Danny Heep flied out. That brought up Lenny Dykstra, the Mets' hustling centerfielder.

Not known as a long ball hitter, Dykstra picked out a Smith forkball and drove it into the rightfield bullpen for a dramatic game-winning home run. The Mets' fans went wild as Dykstra circled the bases. It was a great comeback win and a foreshadowing of things to come. Veteran third baseman Ray Knight called it "the most dramatic win I've ever seen." Was it now time for an encore?

Game four was the Mike Scott Show once again. The big Houston righthander gave up just three hits in taming the New Yorkers for a second time, 3–1. Now the series was tied at two games each with fastballers Nolan Ryan and Dwight Gooden ready to hook up in the pivotal fifth game.

This time, the thirty-nine-year-old Ryan, baseball's all-time strikeout leader, turned back the clock. He was overpowering. Billy Doran drove in a Houston run in the fifth, but when the Mets tied it in their half on a Strawberry homer, a line shot that just got over the fence in the rightfield corner, it was the first hit off Ryan all day.

At the end of nine it was still a 1–1 game. Ryan departed after having given up just two hits and fanning twelve. Gooden pitched through the tenth, and while he was touched for nine hits, gave up just the one run. Now it was up to relievers Charley Kerfeld of Houston and Jesse Orosco of the Mets. Both pitchers had good stuff and by the time the Mets came up in the bottom of the twelfth it was still tied. Then with one out, Wally Backman smashed a single off the third baseman's glove. A pickoff throw went wild and Backman scampered to second. The stage was set.

Kerfeld then walked Keith Hernandez intentionally to set up a possible double play and get to catcher Gary Carter, who was mired in an 0–17 slump. Only this time Carter came through, drilling a Kerfeld fastball to center for a clear hit. Backman raced home with the winning run and the Mets had won a second game in dramatic fashion, 2–1. And while they now had a 3–2 lead in the series, they still viewed the sixth game as big. For if they lost, they would have to deal with Mike Scott once again in the seventh game.

Bob Ojeda and Bob Knepper were the sixth game starters. No one knew it then, but this contest was about to take the series to new dramatic heights. Ojeda got off to a shaky start and the Astros touched him for three in the first. Meanwhile, Knepper was coasting, and kept coasting. Going to the ninth and final inning, he still had his 3–0 lead. The Astros were just three outs away from tying the series. Three outs away!

The first Met batter was pesky Lenny Dykstra, this time in a pinch-hitting role. Knepper was still on the mound, hoping to complete his pitching gem. Dykstra, however, dug in and slammed a triple to right center. Mookie Wilson promptly singled him home and the Mets were on the board. A Kevin Mitchell ground-out sent Mookie to second and he scored on a double by Hernandez. Exit Knepper; enter Dave Smith.

Smith didn't find the going any easier. He walked Carter and Strawberry to load the bases. Ray Knight then lofted a sacrifice fly to right and the game was tied. Smith got out of the inning, but the Mets had done it again. Now the game went to extra innings and became an epic battle.

The game stayed even until the fourteenth. Then the Mets tallied on a single, walk, fielder's choice, and clutch base hit by Wally Backman. The New York bullpen had been mowing the Astros down and Jesse Orosco took over to close it out. But with one out,

110

Houston's Billy Hatcher slammed a home run down the leftfield line. The fans went wild as the Astros, remarkably, had tied it again. So the game continued.

In the sixteenth, the Mets struck once more. A Strawberry double and Ray Knight single brought one home. A pair of wild pitches enabled a second run to score, and a third came in on a single by Dykstra. At 7–4, it once again seemed over. Yet the Astros wouldn't quit. With one out in the home half, Davey Lopes walked and Billy Doran singled. A single by Hatcher scored Lopes and with two out a Glenn Davis single scored Doran. It was now 7–6 with Kevin Bass up. Could the Astros tie it again?

Orosco bore down. He began feeding Bass sharp breaking curves and he finally won the battle. Bass struck out. The sixteen-inning game was over, and the pennant belonged to the Mets. They had won in six games, three of which were heart-stopping in the way they ended.

"My knees are still shaking," Ray Knight said when it ended. And Wally Backman added, "If I was a parent watching my kid play in this game, I'd have had a heart attack in the stands."

Said Knight later, "I've never been involved in anything so emotional and under such a mental strain and under such physical pressure as I have been in this series."

How could anything top that? Well, for starters, take a look at the Boston-California series in the American League. It didn't begin as if it could rival the Mets-Astros for excitement. The Angels won the first game easily, jumping all over Red Sox superpitcher Roger Clemens (24–4 in the regular season) and winning 8–1 behind Mike Witt. In the second game it was the Bosox who won handily, 9–2, with lefty Bruce Hurst the winning pitcher. The teams then moved from Boston to California for the third game.

It started getting tight in Game Three. The Red Sox pitched the emotional Dennis "Oil Can" Boyd against John "Candy Man" Candelaria. Boston drew first blood in the opening inning as catcher Rich Gedman singled home leftfielder Jim Rice. It stayed that way until the sixth when Mr. October, the great Reggie Jackson, singled home rookie Wally Joyner with the tying run.

Now it was the Angels' turn to take the lead. With two out in the seventh, shortstop Dick Schofield homered, catcher Bob Boone singled, and centerfielder Gary Pettis slammed a four-bagger. Suddenly, it was a 4–1 ballgame. The Sox got a pair back in the eighth, but a California insurance run in their half of the inning made it a 5–3 finale. The underdog Angels now had a 2–1 lead in the series.

The next game was another cliffhanger. The Angels winning in the eleventh inning, 4–3, after tying it with three in the ninth, giving the Californians an almost insurmountable 3–1 lead in the playoff series. Game Five in Anaheim matched Bruce Hurst and Mike Witt, and this one also turned into one of the most memorable games in baseball history.

As with most great games, the tension built slowly. In the second, the Red Sox got a pair on a Jim Rice single and a Rich Gedman home run. The Angels came back with a single run in the third, then took the lead in the sixth. With two out, Doug DeCinces doubled and Bobby Grich slammed a long drive to deep left center.

112

Centerfielder Dave Henderson raced to the wall, leaped, and appeared to make a great catch. But as he came down, his glove hit the top of the fence and the ball popped out . . . and over the fence for a home run! The California fans went wild. It was now a 3–2 game.

In the seventh, the Angels picked up a pair of insurance runs to make it 5–2. They were just six outs away from reaching the World Series for the first time in the history of the franchise. Minutes later they were just three outs away when the Red Sox came up for their final turn at bat. Mike Witt was still on the mound, as once again he had pitched brilliantly.

Bill Buckner led things off for the Sox and promptly singled. Witt bore down and struck out the ever-dangerous Jim Rice. Angels fans breathed a sigh of relief. Now, designated hitter Don Baylor was up. Baylor got a Witt fastball and pickled it into the leftfield seats. A two-run homer and it was suddenly a 5–4 game. Witt then rebounded to get Dwight Evans on a pop-up. Two outs, one to go. Now catcher Gedman was up.

That's when Angels' manager Gene Mauch made a move. Since Gedman already had three hits off Witt, he brought in lefty Gary Lucas, who had a history of striking Gedman out. So what happened? Lucas's first pitch hit Gedman, putting him on first. Exit Lucas; enter Donnie Moore, the club's righthanded relief ace. Now Dave Henderson was up. Moore ran the count to 2–2. The Sox were down to their final strike. The champagne was out in the Angels' locker room and police got ready to keep the celebrating crowds off the playing field.

Moore delivered and Henderson swung. CRACK! It was a long drive to leftfield and it . . . was . . . gone! A dramatic home run. Henderson danced around the bases. The man who had let Bobby Grich's homer bounce off his glove had atoned and given the Red Sox a miraculous 6–5 lead. That was the score going into the bottom of the ninth.

With Bob Stanley pitching, Bob Boone led off with a single. Ruppert Jones ran for him and was sacrificed to second by Pettis. Lefty Joe Sambito took over the pitching and Rob Wilfong singled to right, scoring Jones. The Angels had tied it! Now, they wanted to win it. Righty Steve Crawford came in and was greeted by a Dick Schofield single, Wilfong taking third. Brian Downing was then given an intentional walk to load the bases. Amazingly, Crawford got out of it by getting DeCinces and Grich. The game would go to extra innings.

Donnie Moore was still pitching in the eleventh. He started by hitting Baylor with a pitch. Evans then singled Baylor to second, and a bunt single by Gedman loaded the bases. Once again Dave Henderson came up. This time he hit a sacrifice fly to center, scoring Baylor with the go-ahead run. Though the Angels got out of the inning without further damage, it was enough. Calvin Schiraldi retired the Angels in order. The Red Sox had come from one strike away to win it!

It was a gut-wrenching ballgame, so similar to the baseball played by the Mets and Astros in the National League Playoffs. Bobby Grich spoke for everyone when he said, "I'm just drained emotionally. . . . We had it wrapped up, then lost it. It was a tough loss. But what a game, though. Tremendous!"

Unfortunately for the Angels, they never seemed to

recover from being so close. The Red Sox blew them away in Games Six and Seven, 10–4 and 8–1. From being one strike away from elimination, the Red Sox had made it to the World Series against the Mets. Now the question was whether the Series could possibly attain the dramatic heights that had been reached in both Playoff Series. It seemed impossible. The Series, many thought, would be an anticlimax.

Indeed, it took a while for the real action to heat up. Though the Mets were big favorites, the Sox took the first game in New York, Bruce Hurst besting Ron Darling, 1–0, in Game One. The Sox then won the second, 9–3, as both starters, Roger Clemens and Dwight Gooden, were ineffective. When the Series moved to Fenway Park, the Mets battled back, winning 7–1 behind Bob Ojeda and Roger McDowell. They tied it the next night, 6–2, with Ron Darling beating Al Nipper.

Though the Series was now knotted it had yet to produce the drama and hair-raising excitement of the Playoffs. Even the pivotal fifth game was fairly routine. The Sox led all the way and won it 4–2, with Bruce Hurst going the distance. Now it was back to New York for Game Six, and this time the Bosox were out to wrap it up.

They couldn't ask for more than a well-rested Roger Clemens on the mound to face the Mets' Bob Ojeda. And when Ojeda got off to a shaky start, the Sox jumped on him for single runs in the first and second. They were on their way. But Ojeda settled down and the New Yorkers came back in the fifth when Darryl Strawberry walked, stole second, and scored on a single by Ray Knight, the first hit off Clemens. A Mookie Wilson single sent Knight to second and he went to third when rightfielder Dwight Evans bobbled the ball. Then, as pinch hitter Danny Heep banged into a double play, Knight scored the tying run.

It stayed that way until the seventh when the Sox pushed across a run off reliever Roger McDowell, though the run was unearned, scoring as the result of Knight's throwing error. But it gave the Sox the lead and put them just nine outs away from the World Championship.

In the eighth, the Sox had relief ace Calvin Schiraldi in the game, hoping he could close it down. But pinch hitter Lee Mazzilli started things off with a single. Len Dykstra sacrificed him to second and was safe at first on a fielder's choice. A Wally Backman sacrifice moved them up, and Keith Hernandez received an intentional walk to load the bases. Gary Carter's sacrifice fly brought the tying run home.

The Mets almost won it in the ninth, getting the first two runners on, but Schiraldi bore down and retired the side. With Rick Aguilera on the mound for the Mets in the tenth, Boston made its move. Dave Henderson duplicated his clutch hitting in the Playoffs by blasting a home run to give the Sox the lead. And before the smoke cleared, a Wade Boggs double and Marty Barrett single brought home an insurance tally. It was now a 5–3 game and the Mets were down to their final three outs.

With a chance to close it out, Schiraldi went to his fastball. The first two batters, Wally Backman and Keith Hernandez hit lazy fly balls to the outfield. Shea

Stadium was hushed as Gary Carter stepped to the plate. The Mets were down to their final out. It looked as if the World Series would be over in a matter of seconds.

But Carter dug in, determined not to be the final out. He fought off Schiraldi's best stuff and singled to left. A glimmer of hope. Now rookie Kevin Mitchell was up as a pinch hitter. He had had a fine season, but was only three-for-twenty as a pinch swinger. Only this time he came through, punching a single to center, and the Mets had the tying runs on base. But there were still two out.

Third baseman Ray Knight was next. This time Schiraldi had the upper hand as the first two pitches were strikes. Suddenly, the Red Sox were just one strike away, just as the California Angels had been. Could history repeat? Knight said later that he had no fear.

"I've heard that concentration is the ability to think of nothing," he said. "That's what I felt. I was just trying to make contact."

Schiraldi tried an inside fastball and Knight made contact, muscling the pitch to center for a single. Carter scored and Mitchell raced to third. The Mets were within one, but there were still two outs. Boston manager John McNamara yanked Schiraldi in favor of Bob Stanley as switch-hitting Mookie Wilson stepped up. It was to be an at-bat to remember.

Wilson was batting lefthanded and Stanley tried to stay inside on him. Only he went too far inside and Wilson did an acrobatic leap to get out of the way. Catcher Gedman couldn't reach the ball and it rolled to

117

The Mets' Mookie Wilson does some aerial acrobatics to avoid being hit by a Bob Stanley pitch during the sixth game of the 1986 Series. Wilson's agility resulted in a wild pitch that allowed the tying run to score. Moments later, Mookie's grounder to first got through Bill Buckner's legs, and Ray Knight raced home with the gamewinner.

The New York Mets' Howard Johnson (20) greets teammate Ray Knight (22), who races home with the winning run that enabled the New Yorkers to win Game Six of the 1986 World Series against the Boston Red Sox. The Mets were just one strike away from elimination when they rallied to win the game in one of baseball's great moments.

the backstop for a wild pitch as Mitchell scampered home with the tying run, Knight taking second. Now Shea Stadium was in an absolute uproar.

Stanley and Wilson battled for nine pitches, the first eight resulting in three balls and five fouls. Finally, with the count locked at 3–2, Wilson hit a slow dribbler down the first base line. Could he beat it out? First baseman Bill Buckner bent down to field the ball and came up empty. It had gone through his legs! Wilson was safe and Ray Knight raced all the way around to score the winning run. The Mets had done it. They had come from one strike away to tie the Series at three games apiece.

A day of rain only built the drama. It also gave John McNamara a chance to use his most effective pitcher, Bruce Hurst, in the seventh game. The Mets countered with Ron Darling, who had been their best so far. Now it was one game for all the marbles.

In the second, the Sox showed they weren't ready to fold. Dwight Evans led off and rapped a 3–2 pitch over the left centerfield wall for a home run. When catcher Gedman followed with another homer, Mets fans began to worry. A walk, a sacrifice bunt, and a two-out single by Wade Boggs gave the Bosox a third run.

Though Darling settled down after that, Manager Davey Johnson lifted him in the fourth as soon as the Sox threatened. In came lefty Sid Fernandez, who had been dropped from the starting rotation in the Playoffs and Series. Fernandez was brilliant, blowing the Sox away with his fastball and off-speed curves through the sixth inning. That's when the Mets finally got to Hurst.

Lee Mazzilli, pinch hitting for Fernandez, slapped a single to left. A Mookie Wilson single sent Maz to second, and a walk to Tim Teufel loaded the bases. Keith Hernandez then drove in a pair with a single. A Gary Carter fly to right fell out of Dwight Evans' glove when he dove for it and while Hernandez was forced at second, the tying run crossed the plate. It was now anybody's game and anybody's Series.

In the seventh, the Red Sox brought in Calvin Schiraldi once again. The big righty, who had been a bullpen savior for the Sox the second half of the season, didn't have it again and the Mets jumped all over him. Ray Knight started it with a long home run to left center. Len Dykstra smashed a pinch single and went to second on a wild pitch. A Rafael Santana base hit scored Dykstra, and a sacrifice got Santana to second. With Joe Sambito pitching, two walks and a Keith Hernandez sacrifice fly got a third run home. By the time Bob Stanley got the third out the Mets had a 6–3 lead and were close to the championship.

But it was a tribute to the Red Sox that they didn't fold. As had been the pattern throughout the Playoffs and Series, no team could be counted out if there was a strike remaining. In the eighth, the Sox scored two runs, and Jesse Orosco had to bail out Roger McDowell with the tying run on second and none out. But Orosco got Gedman, Henderson, and Baylor, all dangerous hitters, and pitched out of the jam.

Then in the eighth the Mets got insurance. Darryl Strawberry broke a personal Series drought with a long home run. A single by Knight, a groundout, intentional walk, and base hit by pitcher Orosco got a second run home. That made it 8–5, and when Orosco retired the Sox in order in the ninth, it was over. At last. The Mets were world champions.

But what a postseason it had been. The Mets had defeated Houston by a whisker in an emotionally draining series. The Red Sox were a strike away from elimination when they rallied to beat California. And the Mets then became just the third team in baseball history to pull out a World Series victory after being three outs away from elimination. Three outs! Heck. They, too, were just one strike away. It can't get any closer than that.

Bill Gutman has been an avid sports fan ever since he can remember. A freelance writer for fourteen years, he has done profiles and bios of many of today's sports heroes. Although Mr. Gutman likes all sports, he has written mostly about baseball and football. Currently, he lives in Poughquag, New York, with his wife, two step-children, seven dogs and five birds.